SCH
LIBI

BOOK NO.

CLASS

Lynda Waterhouse lives in Elephant and Castle, South London.

When she's not working, she likes lying down, reading magazines and eavesdropping on conversations for research purposes. Her hobbies include missing aerobics classes, watching silent movies and listening to anti-folk music.

LYNDA WATERHOUSE

CUT OFF

Piccadilly Press • London

First published in Great Britain in 2007
by Piccadilly Press Ltd,
5 Castle Road, London NW1 8PR

Text copyright © Lynda Waterhouse, 2007

A catalogue record for this book is available from
the British Library

ISBN-13: 978 1 85340 869 4 (trade paperback)

1 3 5 7 9 10 8 6 4 2

Printed by Creative Print and Design, Wales
Set in Sabon and Fineprint
Cover design by Simon Davis

To my ever patient husband,
David Harris

Diary Room of the Imagination

Mrs Berry says that before you begin any piece of writing you must know your audience. The fact that I have no idea who you are, or if you even exist at all, helps me a lot. I just have this urge to try and make some sense of it all.

Mrs Berry also recommends that you begin at the beginning and work your way systematically to the end. But for me this experience is smashed up like my mum's Georgian glass fruit bowl. Each shard is dangerous and beautiful like a diamond. Some of the pieces are my story, some of them belong to my sister, Vix, and some of them belong to Nan.

Are you sure that you want to fit all the pieces together? I used to think that I would be happy if only I could figure everything out, but over this year I've learned that whoever said that knowledge is power was so wrong.

Knowledge is terror.

Once you know something, unless you are lucky enough to receive a 'forgetting' blow to the head, you are stuck with that knowledge for ever.

Some people discover hidden depths of courage and self-sacrifice and they go on to perform heroic deeds. They pull a stranger from a burning car wreck or they stand up to an oppressive regime.

Some people are too afraid to do the right thing so they just buckle like glass in extreme heat. Others simply . . . cut off. They spend the rest of their lives jumping up and down trying to catch hold of their feelings that are always bobbing just out of reach above their heads.

So here, on this hot October day, I am in the diary room of my imagination, downloading my thoughts and memories and wondering what sort of person I'll turn out to be. Hero? Buckler? Bobber? I need to know the answer because today is a big day for us.

Ava Broadhurst-Conti

Victoria Broadhurst-Conti

Alarm didn't wake me
No familiar arms
To nudge and shake me
Cos I'm now alone
In a houseful of people
Who watch me
When I'm not looking
Who stick up rotas
About dusting and cooking
Who fragrance the place with disinfectant
Not aromatherapy oil
Who call me Victoria
Not Vix
To them I'm a problem
They're trying to fix
But I won't be broken
Today is a big day
I open my bedside cabinet
It's time to take out

My journal
And read it one more time
Float on a kind of nostalgia
Ava has made me a
1960s cocktail dress
Shiny and sleeveless
That's the test
'Me. Me ask about me?'
Has to be suppressed
Can I feel good and not
Bleed in my need to be the best?

Ava

BIG DAY TODAY.

I was running late, as usual, but when I walked past the cathedral something drew me inside.

The blast of cool air gave me goose pimples and my eyes struggled to adjust to the change in the light. As I smoothed my dress, my finger caught on a stray pin and the prickle of pain jolted me. I had only finished adjusting it late last night. I was determined to finish it so I could wear one of Nan's dresses today.

The cathedral was surprisingly crowded. There were groups of tourists alongside people kneeling and praying. Some people were dropping coins into a box and lighting candles. Were they asking for things for themselves, like with wishes on a birthday cake? Wishes can be like volatile radioactive chemicals. People can be too. The right mix of people at the wrong time can do a lot of damage. Today it felt like I had been given the chance to make things right.

A mobile went off close by me, reminding me that I really should be leaving. There was still a lot of stuff to get ready. In a few hours' time, a lot of people would be coming to the café to look at my exhibition. Tasha, my boss at the Cakewalk, would be wondering where I was. I imagined her pacing the small café, brown eyes blazing as she barked orders to Len, who would not be paying her the slightest bit of attention. From this distance they seemed like a comedy act in a surreal sitcom.

I'm not religious or anything, but before I left I decided to light three skinny candles: one for my big sister, Vix, one for me and one for Nan. The flames flickered back at me like the eyes of an understanding friend.

Sooner or later I would have to confess my part in things.

It all began a year ago.

One Year Ago

Vix

Scented gel
Rollerball
The guilt-making charity freebie pen
That screams for help down its side
Or the gushing fountain
Cheeky powder-puff-pink-fluffy-topped one
I have to choose the right weapon
To write my life
Turn it into
The lyrics for a song
That will never be downloaded
Produced or promoted
It's just for me
And as this creation will never be seen
I reserve the right to be as naff and/or mean
As I really am
To speak the words that are closest to my soul
To speak in metaphor and sometimes to rhyme
Because poetry

Doesn't speak in sentences
And as life sometimes imitates art
(That's what makes it a success)
I can talk about myself in this form
In tantalising lines
Cos it's the only way to tell you
My thoughts
And not out loud
Never out loud
I'm a deep thinker
Swallowing ideas and opinions
Like a binge drinker
And because I can dress to impress
Have a card that says American Express
Come from a good family
To look at me you would
Never suspect
That somewhere deep in me is
This need
To confess
Because my life is such
A mixed-up
Crazy mess

Ava

It was the second week of term and I was happily being carried along by the lava flow of girls making their way down the school corridor when Mrs Berry popped out of her office, tapped me on the shoulder and demanded, 'What are you, Ava?'

I twitched and blinked whilst Mrs Berry glanced impatiently at her clipboard. The question sounded odd, like something out of a Shakespeare play. Had I heard it right? She knew perfectly well who I was, but what I was? That was a truly bizarre question. Mrs Berry was always emphasising what she called 'appropriateness in partnership with academic achievement'. I chewed the inside of my cheek and debated whether to put on a mockney accent and say something sassy like, 'A lot prettier and richer than you, darlin'.' She ran the philosophy club so perhaps my answer should've been something along the lines of, 'What I am, Mrs Berry, is a product of my own upbringing. Nothing more, nothing less.'

I come from an interesting family background. My dad comes from a long line of Welsh/Italian ice cream makers.

Grandpa Conti created the award-winning 'Welsh Rarebit' flavour. Dad's tastes were even weirder – he left the world of ice cream for the tang of politics.

My mother, Elspeth Broadhurst-Conti, is a barrister who spends her days arguing for people's rights and her nights pointing out all my wrongs. We didn't know much about her father, apart from the fact that he came from Africa and met Nan whilst he was studying law in Manchester and went back unexpectedly, leaving her expecting! Mum refuses to talk about him but is determined to become a high court judge. How twisted is that?

Mrs Berry cleared her throat and tapped her pen impatiently. I am down on some sort of list as having non-specific learning difficulties (no one can actually specify what they are!) so she was obviously giving me more time. Nan had argued with Mum about it saying, in her Manchester accent, 'She only seems slow in your household because the rest of you are always dashing about like headless chickens.'

What was I? The answer to this question would have to be, 'A great disappointment to my family'. It was my big sister, Victoria, who had been visited in her cot by the fairy godmother and granted the classic girlie-girl wishes of being the Pretty One *and* the Clever One.

I had all the same features as my sister – long dark wavy hair, brown eyes, but whereas people talked about her 'Julia Roberts smile', I felt like a wide-mouthed-frog.

People said she was curvy and had an hourglass figure; I resembled a barometer – thin neck and big bottom.

Mrs Berry broke the silence. 'Now, shall I put you down as Other? I usually do put you and Victoria down as that but I thought I'd better check. This ethnic monitoring form has to be sent off today. Is that fine?' She smiled weakly at me.

I twitched the corners of my mouth back at her.

Mrs Berry quickly ticked a box and scanned the corridor for the next person on her list.

I rejoined the lava flow and made my way to morning assembly where I tried to forget about how weird that conversation had made me feel.

How 'Other'.

Vix

In September
I shrieked with delight when I saw her
In the corridor
She shrieked too
And waved her arms
We hugged
Rosamund
My template
My one true model
For a bezzie mate
I squealed and said
'You're looking . . .'
I paused
Her presence filled the gap
Down to size zero, teeth been changed by brace
Brunette is the new blond
'And you Vix,'
She looks me full in the face
'You're just the same.'

Ava

After that weird conversation with Mrs Berry I couldn't wait to get to my textiles class. Once I've got a needle in my hand rather than a pen I can relax. Miss Duncan shares my interest in vintage fabrics. Ever since I can remember, I've been collecting old Barbie dolls and designing outfits for them. Over the last few years I have been scouring charity shops and car boot sales for old dress patterns and then trying to find the right scraps of vintage fabrics to recreate them in miniature. My family call them my Bootsale Barbies. When I'm sewing or following a dress pattern I don't feel clumsy and my ideas flow.

Mum had been questioning me about my course-work over dinner the other night when Vix had cut in, 'Isn't textiles a term of abuse?'

'Only if you're a naturist and don't wear any clothes,' Mum had replied and then they'd laughed.

To them textiles was a soft option. Not something to be taken seriously. To me it was everything. The textiles room was my sanctuary. It's the only room in the whole school where I actually feel that I can do something.

I can totally sympathise with people who say they are trapped in the wrong body – I am trapped in the wrong family and so have been sent to the wrong school for me. Somewhere out there is a super brainy girl trapped in a family of dullards.

The lesson was spent with Miss Duncan outlining the personal portfolio element of our course.

'As there are only four of you taking this course, you will be expected to get on and work independently. You will have free access to the room and some of your classes will be shared with the other A-level and GCSE students. I'm really looking forward to working with you. You will have the opportunity to take up a work experience module to gain valuable practical knowledge and I will say more about that as the term progresses, but enough of this talking – over to your sewing machines . . .'

Music to my ears!

Then in walked Rosamund's sister, Kennedy.

Vix

Baudelaire had green hair
He liked loose-living women
In their underwear
Christopher Marlowe
Liked boys and tobacco
And spying
I have a mind
That in its
Private moments
Thinks in
Cheap rhymes
Often
When I'm scared
It's like I have this
Large tape measure
Stuck down my spine
And reaching above my head
I try to stretch
But I never quite measure
Up

No one can see this
Only me
Wish I could be
More like my moon-faced sister
Let off the hook
With her weird love of textiles
And textures to caress
The sister that Mum insists
Must be given time
To process
Her thoughts
We are total opposites
That don't attract

Ava

I used to watch my sister like I was playing a game at a kid's birthday party. The one where you have to memorise the objects on a tray. I thought that by doing that I would discover the secrets of how to be popular, clever and well groomed. That some of the fairy dust would rub off on me.

So far, all I had learned from my sister was that you had to spend hours in the bathroom, shriek on the phone to your friends, act like a bored thirty-something in bars that you are only just legally allowed in, have incomprehensible conversations about obscure architects or designers and pout like a three-year-old when you don't get your own way.

Vix could interrupt one of our heavy family political debates about war or poverty saying, 'You know what . . . If I'm being honest, I don't really care what happens on the news. It doesn't really affect me.'

Everyone would laugh and comment on how arch and ironic she was. Mum would have signed me up on the spot for a world awareness class if I had said that.

I would have liked to talk over my 'Other' feelings with my sister, but Rosamund and her sister Kennedy had come back to Hildegard School and Vix went from being Ms Just About Bearable to Ms Totally Impossible.

Rosamund always had this effect on her. Brought out her pretentious side. Nothing was ever good enough after she'd spent an evening with Rosamund, especially not me. When Rosamund was not around we would meet together in the evenings and share a hot chocolate and chat about stuff. Nothing earth-shattering, but we would talk or sometimes watch a soppy DVD together.

Lately it seemed that Rosamund was always hanging around – being ultra charming and faintly bored in the background.

To me Rosamund has always smelled wrong. She was too plastic perfect, like one of the Bootsale Barbies that I collect. No one can always say and do the right thing. Not without following a script instead of their own feelings. And Vix was starting to smell wrong too. There was no time in her life for anyone else apart from Rosamund.

Rosamund and her sister Kennedy had always lived across the square from us but had spent the last few years away trying out a couple of boarding schools. Since the start of term, when Vix took up with Rosamund and the broadband brain brigade, she had dropped most of her former friends.

Mum hadn't been too keen on the friendship but that

all changed when Vix was invited to join the G+T club. To be labelled gifted and talented at Hildegard School is really something because nearly everyone there has a super-sized brain to start with. Vix had always been just hovering on the outer rings of this group, so when she was selected to join the crème de la crème that was the end of all questions about their friendship.

Kennedy and I were not expected to be friends. Not since I had melted her Barbie Dream Castle after she had tricked me into drinking her special French lemonade (*oui-oui*). Kennedy loved playing practical jokes on me. She seemed to think making me look a fool was the funniest thing on the planet. Over the years I'd learned it was easier to stay out of her way.

She is not as smart as Rosamund but she is ten times pushier. She was the one who always got to play Mary in the Nativity play at primary school whilst I was third sheep or the messenger with one line. She was causing a stir at school already by requesting to bring her lapdog Precious into class with her. Mrs Berry had turned beetroot at that suggestion and muttered something about appropriateness and allergies. Kennedy had blinked back and said that stroking pets was good for high blood pressure.

Vix

Rosamund has been working her way through
     boarding schools
Understimulated and unchallenged
'A bunch of upper-middle-class fools'
Is how her mother described it to mine
One evening
Over a cup of anti-ageing detoxifying chai tea
Rosamund's mum is selling it
On the packet it says
One thousand women can't be wrong
Mother's arched eyebrow would argue the case
But for once she says nothing
They've known each other
Since we were embryos
Met in Harley Street
When they were both expecting
Pitter patter of baby feet
They did it the second time too
Another two girls
But Kennedy and Ava

They never got on
Don't have that bond
Like me and Rosamund

Rosamund's smart
Her goal in life is to be
Like a work of art
Absolute Perfection
Follow the cool rules
Of the smart set
She is Perpetually Fab
Her life
Meticulously planned
Even down to spending
Several months
In rehab
To always be in the
Going up section of the glossy mag
Never the going down . . .
Unless going down becomes
The new going up
Like black is the new brown
Or it is the other way around?
On the other hand
I am someone who is waiting for her life to start

Ava

Curiosity was like a carbohydrate blow-out for me. I'd get this massive sugar rush of energy from uncovering secrets. Sneaking into places, opening letters or reading e-mails made my heart beat faster and my body tingle with the power of knowing things that other people didn't want me to. Then, after the energy boost had burned itself out, I'd take a long hard look at myself, feel shabby and ashamed, and swear that I would never do anything like that again . . . until the next time.

The urge to snoop would slowly build up like a hot pimple underneath my skin. I would feel restless and pace about the place and then, as if by magic, an opportunity would present itself.

The next opportunity came about a month later.

Dad had a den on the second floor. He called it his office, Mum 'his lair'. It contained a large antique desk, a battered armchair and an old television and video recorder as well as an ancient record player for Dad's prized vinyl collection. I was in there for a legitimate reason – an urgent need for a paper clip or a staple.

Mum had placed a large cardboard box slap bang in the middle of the room and filled it with some of Dad's junk. There was a Post-it note on top saying *DECLUTTER?* Some of the objects in there were ancient videos. One of them was marked, *Graduation.*

Mum was always clearing the house. She hated what she called unnecessary baggage and the rest of us called 'essential stuff'. Dad had even gone as far as rewriting the words to one of his favourite Pink Floyd songs, making us all chant, 'Oi, Elspeth – leave our stuff alone!'

I thought it would be mildly amusing to watch a bit of this video and laugh at the time-warped version of my parents before they got old and successful and had us, so I fished it out of the box and played it.

Dad had obviously taped the ceremony over something because at the beginning was some film taken in a forest. A young, floppy-haired version of Dad was messing around pulling faces at the camera and a woman's voice was yelling instructions at him. Then the film juddered as they swapped places and the woman perched on a rock by the stream. The woman drew her knees up to her chest and looked shyly at the camera as Dad said, 'I love you, Katy. I always will.'

The woman looked up, blinked back and said, 'Love you too, Alan.'

I was just absorbing all of this when Jonathon, our Busy Mate (does the jobs you hate!), came in with a pile of Dad's letters and I quickly turned off the video, picked up a pen and left. One of the downsides of having cash-rich/time-poor parents is that 'help' always surrounds you. Jonathon's pretty cool, despite the fact that he refused to do any of the jobs I hated – like English assignments.

'Are you sure you should be doing that?' Jonathon called after me.

I froze.

He arched an eyebrow. 'Isn't that your dad's Montblanc pen that the Prime Minister gave him?'

Vix

'So what do you think?'
Mrs Berry asks
Then just as
I'm preparing to focus
On someone else's
Clever answer
She adds Victoria
'What do you think, Victoria?'
I sort of know what I think
About Hamlet's indecision
Bad for a hero – good for a human
My thoughts sound loose and flip
And the words are common and trite
Leave it
I'd better seal my words up tight
Rather than sound stupid and crap
Rosamund comes in
With an answer off pat
Quoting an ancient critic
F R Leavis

Ava

I'd never really thought much about my parents' relation-ship. You're only supposed to do that if you're in therapy or are writing one of those 'misery' biographies about your unspeakably monstrous parents and how you overcame great odds to be what you are today. Besides, parents don't act like they are in love all the time. That is so wrong.

My parents had met at university and got married soon after they had graduated. Mum was relieved that she had got married early, saying that it allowed her to get her babies out of the way and then channel her energies into her career. Dad was always working and involved in important projects. It was weird to think of him being in love with someone else and I couldn't look at him in the same way. It felt as if he'd betrayed us by not loving Mum as much as someone else.

Dad and I had always been close. The 'Happy Families' pairings in our house were clear – Vix and Mum, Dad and me. For years it had been our ritual that I would sit with him before supper whilst he finished up his work on the laptop. Since I'd watched the video it gave me a strange kind of satisfaction to see how hurt he looked when I made excuses and stayed away.

By the first week of December I had weakened and went to join him at the kitchen table. I'd made us two mugs of hot chocolate, complete with marshmallows and chocolate sprinkles.

He looked up at me and smiled. 'Perfect. Just what I needed after reading that report.'

He was closing the laptop and putting endless papers in his 'longwinded' case when Mum burst in followed by Vix, Rosamund and Kennedy.

Mum was wearing her blue silk coat and dress and her diamonds. She placed a floppy bouquet of deep red roses down on the table along with a glass bowl.

'A very rare example of Georgian crystal. The senior partner gave it to me in recognition of all my work this year.'

'This calls for Champagne,' Dad said, jumping up and taking a bottle from the fridge.

'It's a beautiful object,' Rosamund gushed.

'Shall I put the roses in a vase?' Kennedy picked them up. 'Is that hot chocolate, Ava?'

'I hope not before supper.' Mum grabbed a mug and her nose twitched. 'And what have I told you about all this sugary nonsense on top?'

'My mum says white sugar makes you rot,' Kennedy added.

'I'm not sure about that, but it certainly fills you up before your evening meal,' Mum said, scooping up the mugs and placing them on the draining board.

Dad winked at me. 'I asked Ava to make it for me.'

I shot him a grateful look.

Vix groaned. 'Sure you did.'

Mum gazed at the bowl. 'I'm completely stunned by this. It's so beautiful. Look how it catches the light. I'm going to put it in the sitting room and I shall fill it with seasonal fruit. I think I'll start with some Kent apples.'

She carried it ceremoniously out of the room. Mum was a sucker for antiques. She had been brought up single-handedly by Nan in Manchester so there hadn't been much spare cash around. She was certainly making up for it now.

Kennedy sipped her Champagne beside me and said, 'Your mum is very smart.'

I braced myself for the next line . . . *Shame you are so dumb!* Kennedy had one of those naturally sarcastic voices. Instead she asked, 'Do you want to come to a yoga class with me?'

My brain was still processing this information and how to respond to it when she continued, 'It's on a Saturday morning.'

Relief flooded through me as I tried to look disappointed. 'I work at the Cakewalk café on Saturdays,' I told her.

'It's a great class but you can't eat for three hours

30

beforehand,' Rosamund added. 'Too much pressure on the stomach.'

'I'll go,' Vix said.

Vix

Rosamund and I have been making plans
For our perfect life
A road map for all the great things to come
To kick start all that
I'm taking the option of
Three A-levels, one AS with
Extended curriculum option
A baccalaureate
Chavs and losers
Waifs and strays are the ones
Who get the plain A's
For me it has to be
A first class degree
At Oxford
Jobs working in New York and Japan
With weekend shopping breaks in Paris and Milan
Topped off by a
Passionate love affair with famous married man
Then settle down with some minor aristocrat with
        drop-dead gorgeous looks

Who exhibits his sculptures all round the world
Throw in two kids and during a career break
Knock out
Some bestselling children's books
Finding the time to be a pedagogue
To all the world
With my witty blog
How light and simple it all sounds
Light and simple
For someone else
Who isn't weak
And loathsome like me
And yet
If you want something badly enough it has to
    happen
Doesn't it?

Ava

During my next visit to Dad's den I nudged the mouse and noticed that Dad had not signed off from his e-mail account. I clicked on the most recent e-mail and found myself reading it. If my eyes just happened to flick along the screen there would be no harm in that would there?

My Dear Alan
    I can't tell you how good it is to make contact with you again. I have always felt bad about the way things ended between us. There's never an easy way to say goodbye to someone you love is there? Especially when other people are involved.

The hairs on the back of my neck prickled. It sounded like Dad had been having an affair! I read on.

    Sometimes I still feel exactly like the person I once was when we were so close and I long to drink whisky and talk with

you until the early hours of the morning
or until the world has been put right. I
yearn to dress up in outlandish clothes
and dance in a preposterous fashion at a
student ball. I know that you would insist
that what I'm wearing now is preposterous
enough.

Listen to me! It's just that I was
feeling a bit low and I heard an old song
on the radio, saw your name on a press
release and decided to contact you. It
meant so much to me that you replied and
took the time to tell me all your news.

I am so impressed by the brilliant
careers that you and Elspeth have carved
out for yourselves and the beautiful
children you have created. Your daughters
sound so different from one another. You
must be very proud of them.

So Dad had been telling this person all about us.

I would love to meet them and to see you
and Elspeth again.

My last bout of malaria has left me
feeling low. I warn you that this trip
will be a make or break one for me in

terms of the course of my life in the
future. So no pressure then!

Looking forward to seeing you all in the
summer.

Here's hoping that my prayers don't land
on stony ground.

With love, Sister Catherine aka Katy XXX

The woman from the video! The one that had looked at
Dad like he was a superhero and said that she loved him
so much. Then another thought punched into my brain.
Dad had been in love with a nun. YUCK!

On impulse, I pressed the reply button and wrote
quickly.

Not any space for you to stay. Elspeth.

It was only when the message, *Your e-mail has been sent*
flashed up on the screen and I clicked on OK that it sank
in. Things were definitely not OK because I'd broken the
first rule of snooping. NEVER INTERFERE. If you interfere then you draw attention to yourself. And if you draw
attention to yourself then people become more closed up.
I tried telling myself that Mum would thank me one day
for sending that e-mail and saving her marriage.

Vix

Take those three black girls on the bus
Sitting in front of me
Comparing their skin
To see who is the lightest one
Rubbing and pressing down on each other's arms
Then they look over at me
And whisper something
And laugh
I sit up and look out of the window
Check my messages on my phone
Stick my iPod in
Try not to feel
So ugly and
Alone

Ava

On my way down the high street I passed Salvador's. It didn't look like much from the outside with its old-fashioned wooden panelling and shutters. Pascal, the new owner, had extended it at the back with a modern glass and steel structure that had won loads of architectural prizes and wound up all the old residents in the neighbourhood.

When I got to the café that Saturday, Len was having one of his off days. They were hard to predict but with a bit of questioning you could always find a reason for them, like the anniversary of a battle he'd fought in or his little girl's birthday. We always called Len's daughter a little girl even though she must be over twenty now and has got children of her own.

Years ago, Len had been involved in a war in the Falkland Islands and he'd found it hard to settle after that. His wife divorced him and he started living rough. Then Tasha's father, who had been a colonel in the army, had taken Len in and given him a job at the café.

'I burned the Gucci pies,' Tasha explained as she waved a tea towel in the air.

The Cakewalk was a fashion-themed café and all the dishes are named accordingly. Tasha's father had bought it for her after she'd graduated from art college two years ago. Tasha had transformed the old, triangular-shaped, former ladies' gowns shop into a brilliant café. She'd kept a lot of the original features and used them to display work from the local fashion college. The white walls were often covered with art for sale.

Len cannot bear the smell of smoke. At that moment, he was curled up in the corner of the kitchen with a frozen expression.

'Don't you mean the Gucci crème brûlées,' I joked as I joined in the waving with my apron.

Tasha flicked the tea towel at me. Then she started to haphazardly load the dishwasher, rattling all the pots in a way that she knew really bothered Len. He is a stickler for what he calls 'apple pie order'.

Len jumped up and took over the dishwasher loading duty.

'Leave that to me!' he barked. 'If you want a job doing properly . . .'

Tasha looked grateful and sighed. 'You're a treasure, Len.'

Tasha was a scream to work for. At the moment she had her hair dyed black and cut into a bob and was modelling herself on a silent movie star of the 1920s called Louise Brooks. She was twenty-four and sometimes acted as if she was fourteen. At other times, like when she handled Len's moods, she seemed the wisest person I knew.

As the smoke cleared and the dishwasher hummed, she ordered a cup of tea from Len. 'And make it exactly how I like it!'

'Two sugars,' Len snapped back. 'Some people don't want to take orders from a woman but I'm not like that. I respect the chain of command!'

That's what I liked about the Cakewalk café. There was no such thing as a typical Saturday or a dull moment. Best of all, there are no trick questions at the Cakewalk, just customers who need serving and conversations to be had with Tasha and Len.

When it was quiet, we would all try and invent new recipes for the café or Tasha would entertain us with tales of her days as a fashion student at St Martin's College or Len would sing us country and western songs.

Pascal was always our first customer. He was only twenty-one but he was supremely confident and so physically attractive it was painful to look at him. He had liquid blue eyes and dark hair and perfectly pro-portioned features. Rumour had it that he had been a model for a while. There was also something shambling and charming about him. He was always scrounging roll-ups off Len and his outrageously expensive designer trousers were always crumpled. He called me 'Ava, his luscious lovely' in a way that made me giggle rather than squirm. Even Tasha let him get away with calling her his 'Fragrant flapper!' in reference to her love of 1920s style.

'Some people are just naturals for taking the extra biscuit,' Tasha would say about him. 'He probably doesn't even realise that other people's lives don't coast along.'

Like my sister, I thought as I added, 'He does work hard though.'

'He's even got you defending him!' Tasha wagged her finger.

'Attack is the best form of defence!' Len countered and we all laughed again.

That Saturday morning Kennedy came in with her little dog in a large bag.

'Precious is also called my little Plum because he likes my Mulberry bags best,' she said after she had ordered a large coffee and a slice of Versace sponge. 'I thought I'd come and see you after yoga. Vix and Rosamund had better things to do but I don't. Besides yoga makes us hungry, doesn't it, baby?'

'The dog does yoga?' I asked.

'Oh yes, Precious Plum goes to a separate doggie class.'

'The world's gone mad,' Len said, sniffing.

'Why don't you go and join her for a while?' Tasha

asked, nudging me, when Kennedy had sat down. 'Everybody needs one OAF.'

'What?'

'An own age friend. Someone who has the same cultural references.'

I shook my head. There was too much history between Kennedy and me to make it as friends. Kennedy didn't strike me as the type who would go in for OAFs as she seemed to like spending time with her sister and Vix. I felt a pang of something when I thought about them all hanging round together, having things in common. Not jealousy exactly but something like it. I admire people who can do group things.

Tasha wasn't giving up. 'A person who likes dogs can't be all bad. Besides, I'm getting an idea. How does "Doggy afternoon teas" sound?' Crazy schemes were always popping into Tasha's head.

'Like a weird porn film?' I replied and she nudged me again with her incredibly bony elbow. Tasha is a fierce nudger.

She rolled her eyes. 'The quiet ones are the worst.'

'Do you really think so?' An image of my dad and Katy who was now Sister Catherine flashed into my mind. You can't get much quieter than a nun!

I loosened the strings of the long white apron that Tasha made us wear and sat next to Kennedy.

'This cake is gorgeous,' Kennedy said. 'Isn't it,

Precious?' She fed a large piece to the little white dog.

'Doesn't it feel trapped in there?' I asked.

'Oh no – my little Plummy likes to be all snuggled up, don't you?' Kennedy unzipped the bag and pulled out the tiny dog. 'Besides, I don't want to get dog hairs on my clothes, do I?'

I stared at Kennedy, unsure if I should answer the question or not. I'm not sure if she would have been happy with my answer. Dog hairs go along with the territory of having a dog! That was too obvious, wasn't it?

I decided that it was time to try out my friendship question on her.

'Kennedy. Cathy and Heathcliff from *Wuthering Heights* – what's the first thing you think of?' I asked. It was my integrity test. It really bothers me when people use Cathy and Heathcliff as a classic example of young love. To me, the story is about how an older man takes revenge for his screwed up passions on the next generation. Their children are the ones who have to sort the mess out before they can find love. Anyone who went on about love and passion and star-crossed lovers was marked down as a no-no as a potential good friend.

I was pretty sure that Kennedy would give me an obvious answer, but she surprised me by saying, 'That story really bugs me. Everyone is so mean.'

'Better get back to work,' I said, and I was just edging

off my seat when the door opened and in walked Rosamund and my sister who said, 'Two decaffeinated skinny lattes,' to me as if it was my job in life to wait on her.

'Let's sit over here.' Rosamund indicated the table tucked away in the corner, from which you could see Pascal's wine bar.

Kennedy grinned at me as she joined them.

As Tasha helped me make the lattes she whispered, 'More members of Pascal's fan club.'

'He'd better watch out then,' I said as I poured out the steamed milk. 'They always get what they want.'

'Not what they deserve.' Tasha giggled. 'Oh, I'm so profound.'

'If you say so,' I added and Tasha pretended to look hurt.

'And I was going to give you some time off to go to the St John's autumn jumble sale this afternoon. There's always good pickings there.'

'Sounds like it might be fun.' Kennedy had crept up on us at the counter. 'What time does it start?'

I was about to make up an excuse when Tasha said, 'Two o'clock, but if I let you out for an hour I want you to look out some stuff for me.'

'Great fun.' Kennedy grinned as I handed over the coffee cups to her. I noticed that she paid for all the coffees. 'I'll meet you outside the church.' Then she sat down with Vix and Rosamund who continued chatting to each other.

Maybe Precious wasn't the only lapdog around here, I thought, and felt a pang of pity for Kennedy.

'*Dropkick me, Jesus, through the goalposts of life!*' Len sang from the kitchen.

'Someone is feeling better,' Tasha said, nudging me in the ribs.

'Is that song for real?' I asked.

''Fraid so.'

Ava

I turned up twenty minutes before the jumble sale opened. Nan had taught me that you had to get there early to get the best pickings. 'Better still, try and be one of the helpers. They get to see what everyone has sent in.' Nan was ferocious when it came to getting a bargain, saying, 'Who wants something that is too easy to come by?'

Kennedy was standing right by the entrance and Precious was getting lots of attention from the strict old ladies in charge of the door.

She waved when she saw me. 'What exactly are we looking for?' she asked.

I bristled a little at the 'we' as I shrugged and replied, 'I don't know. Interesting objects. I like to find scraps of old material. Curtain fabric from the 1950s or 1960s. I use them for my miniature doll collection. Where are Rosamund and Vix?' I half expected to see them and braced myself for some comments.

'They've gone to their Oxbridge tutorial and then they are going over to see Pascal about a scheme. I suppose it would be all right to tell you.'

I pretended not to hear as we walked into the hall.

'It's better if we go our separate ways,' I said, walking off in one direction and hoping Kennedy would take the hint.

I was bending down rummaging through a box that was underneath a table when she came rushing up to me.

'Ava, what do you think of this? It's a pound.' She waved a small square of fabric under my nose.

'Not bad,' I said, trying not to show how excited I was. Another of Nan's tips for successful bargain hunting was never to show emotion when handling an interesting item.

'I think she'll take seventy-five pence,' Kennedy whispered in my face. I dipped into my pocket and handed her a coin. It was a swatch of Lucienne Day printed fabric. A real find.

After half an hour's rummaging, I'd only managed to find a 1960s gingham peg bag. 'Are you sure you don't want it?' I offered Kennedy the Lucienne Day fabric as we were leaving.

She screwed up her nose. 'No, it's all yours. I prefer to get my vintage look from designer boutiques but I really enjoyed myself. Some of those old ladies can certainly knock you out of the way.'

'Never underestimate the force of an old lady in search of a bargain,' I said, grinning as we made our way back to the café. As we passed Salvador's, we spotted Vix and Rosamund sitting in the window. Kennedy waved and they gave her a half-hearted nod in return.

Kennedy lowered her voice. 'Now I'm going to tell you what Vix and Rosamund are up to. They are going to try and persuade Pascal to let them hire out his club so that they can hold the prom party there in the summer. It will take lots of organising and persuading but it will be brilliant if it comes off, won't it? We might even get invited to help out.'

I grunted. Helping out was not my idea of fun but I didn't want to hurt Kennedy's feelings.

'I'd better get back to work now,' I said as we reached the Cakewalk. Kennedy sighed and looked a little sad so I added, 'I had a really good time.' I gave her my best 'jumble sales elbows' impression.

Kennedy shrieked. 'You're so funny, Ava. Ever since my mum saw your dad on *Question Time* she's been nagging me to see more of you. She loved that feature about Elspeth in *Marie Claire* too.'

Speechless, I walked back into the café.

Vix

Alarm clock buzz six a.m.
Facial cleansing wipe to remove sleep
Drink hot water and lemon
Body brush and exfoliating cream
Warm shower with aromatherapy oils
Shampoo and conditioner
Cold shower
Body crème and towel dry hair
Dry off, apply deodorant, feminine spray
And light body mist
Rinse hands then apply foaming facial scrub,
Cleanser, tone and moisturise the skin
Tweeze eyebrows
Eat breakfast – warm oatcake and honey
And probiotic vitamin
Floss teeth and brush
Then antibacterial oral rinse
Final sloosh with teeth whitening rinse
Apply light make-up
Eyeliner and mascara

Massage serum into scalp
And blow dry
Take off dressing gown and put on underwear
Make sure that spare pantyliner is in bag
Get dressed
Put on earrings and moisturise hands
Coat of clear nail polish
Check school bag
Read over any homework
Avoid parents
Avoid sister till last minute
Jonathon texts me when the car's ready
Drops me off
For soya latte
At coffee shop
Think that I am just about decent enough
To face the day
'You OK?' Rosamund asks. 'Your mascara's
    smudged.'
'Got up late – I was in a rush.'

Ava

'No one can make you feel inferior without your consent,' Miss Duncan said as we were working on the costumes for the Christmas play the following Monday morning. We were sewing costumes for the drama club's new avant-garde interpretation of Cinderella. It was set in the future and the director had decided that everyone was wearing space costumes.

My thoughts are always clearer when I'm sewing. I feel less pressure to say the right thing when my fingers are holding a needle.

'I'm not sure about that,' I said. 'It's really hard to change people's ideas about you if everyone thinks you're stupid. They might not come out and say it but they show it in all the ways that they respond to you.'

'But you don't have to accept it. You have to tell yourself that you are better than that and follow your own expectations.'

I didn't say anything else or ask any further questions because I knew that I felt inferior because I was. That decent, good people didn't snoop and read other people's e-mails and even worse respond to them pretending to be someone else. Or do what I had done the day before.

It was Jonathon's day off and Irene, our Thai housekeeper, had gone to visit some friends. Vix was over at Rosamund's revising. Dad was at Chequers with the Prime Minister and Mum was meeting an important client so it was up to me to answer the door.

It was a smartly dressed black woman with an envelope in her hand.

'This is the Broadhurst-Contis'?'

I nodded and she nodded at someone in the car waiting and handed me an envelope.

'I have just returned from a trip abroad and Sister Catherine asked me to deliver this to you. The post is so unreliable over there and she knew I was coming to the neighbourhood so she asked me to drop this off.'

After she'd gone I stood for a long time in the hall holding the letter. Sister Catherine had addressed the letter to Mum and Dad. She would certainly have mentioned that e-mail in the letter and I was going to get into so much trouble.

If only somebody else had been in the house; it would have made it so much easier for me to do the right thing and leave the envelope in the hall.

Then another thought struck me. What if this letter was announcing that she was coming back to claim Dad and that Mum's crazy e-mail had helped her to clarify things. Then I would've made things worse.

The back door slammed and Irene called out, 'Yoohoo.'

I ran upstairs to my bedroom and put the letter in my sewing basket.

Towards the end of the lesson Miss Duncan made an announcement. 'I have some news about the work experience programme. It won't be taking place until the end of the summer term, but the placements take time to organise so I'd like you to think about what placement you want with a view to gaining experience in an area you would like to have a career.'

Maybe I should have asked for a placement as a spy.

There was one place that I'd love to work – in the costume department of the Victoria and Albert Museum.

On the way out of class Kennedy asked me, 'Where does that line about not being inferior come from? Miss Duncan is always quoting it at us.'

'Eleanor Roosevelt, I think,' I replied.

'Who's she?'

'Kennedy, you of all people should know about her.'

Kennedy screwed up her face. 'Has she been on the cover of *Vogue*?'

I shook my head and laughed. 'She was the wife of an

American president, *Kennedy*! Remember – your mum named you after one.'

'Oops!'

'What's the big joke, girls?' Miss Duncan asked, which made us laugh all over again.

Ava

The days passed and still the stolen letter stayed in my sewing basket. Every so often I would take it out and look at it, wishing that I had X-ray eyes or a time machine. But no matter how hard I wished, nothing seemed to change. The letter was still there. I couldn't bring myself to open it and I had no idea what to do with it.

School carried on much as usual. The drama department raved about the space age Cinderella costumes. Kennedy had developed the habit of coming in to the Cakewalk after yoga every Saturday, usually followed by Vix and Rosamund who spent their time hoping for Pascal or one of his friends to come in for their afternoon espresso. Sometimes Rosamund's mum would join them. Then she would insist on ordering herbal teas and she would shriek loudest of them all at everything Pascal said.

Tasha was unimpressed. 'To be quite frank about it, I thought that smart girls would act differently. Sometimes it seems that you are the older sister.'

'Have you ever done anything that you're not particularly proud of?' I asked her.

Tasha snorted. 'It would be easier to ask me to list the things I've done that I have been proud of. It would be a shorter list.'

I picked at a piece of stray skin on my lip. 'I suppose you learn by your mistakes.'

'Hah!' Tasha's eyes flashed. 'A nice sentiment, but from my experience, once you have made a mistake the world can be a very unforgiving place. How many years have you been at Hildegard? How do they deal with "failures"?'

I shook my head. 'Not an option.'

'And look at Len. He's been in a war and over twenty years later he can't get over whatever terrible mistake it was that he made. How does society treat him? I'd be very careful about owning up to any mistakes if I were you. No matter what they say, Hildegard people see it as a sign of weakness.' She pulled out a small notebook from her apron. 'Now we have to put our brains together on the small matter of Pascal's birthday cake.'

He was planning a big party to promote the club as well as celebrating his birthday.

'I'm thinking a novelty cake for him in the shape of his bar,' I said after a while.

'Ava, that's a brilliant idea! Gives us a perfect excuse to go in and check the place out too. I'm dying to see how he's changed the interior.'

After my conversation with Tasha, I decided that I

would simply take the letter and drop it on the mat the next morning; wipe the whole experience from my mind and deny all knowledge of it if anyone asked.

But it was the next morning that we received the phone call.

Nan had been taken into hospital.

Ava

As we pulled up outside the small terraced house, it started to drizzle. Mum tapped the steering wheel with her paper-thin leather driving gloves and sighed dramatically.

'An Italian sunset makes you gasp at its beauty and Manchester rain makes you desperate to escape.'

I stared out of the window. Vix had been too snowed under with work to come. If she'd been in the car with Mum there would have been a stream of non-stop banter, at least one row and lots of screeching laughter.

But I am not Vix.

'Ava, are you clear about what you're doing? Just leave the brochure lying around and say that we *all* think it's a good idea. Remember that it is a retirement complex and not just sheltered accommodation.'

I swallowed and nodded. There was no point arguing with Mum once she'd got an idea in her head.

'I'm on the mend,' Nan declared to me as we drank tea in the living room. Mum was busy scrubbing out the kitchen. Mum claimed that the heat of Nan's gas fire was too much for her and yet she would happily pay a small fortune to go to her 'hot yoga' class in London. Mum and Nan rubbed each other up the wrong way.

I spent a lot of time staring into the fake flames of the gas fire. There's nothing like being told that you have to say something for making the conversation section of your brain clam up.

'Have a biscuit.' Nan thrust a plate of chocolate Digestives at me.

After I'd stuffed one in my mouth she demanded some news so, through a mesh of crumbs, I told her, 'Vix is planning on going to Oxford. She's really pleased because Rosamund has been called for an interview, too.'

Nan sniffed. 'Never liked that girl. Eyes too close together, just like her mother.'

I giggled. 'Nan! You can't say things like that!'

She dipped her biscuit in her tea. 'It's only my way of saying that there is something about that girl that I don't trust. Every time I've met her over the years she was too well behaved – too bloody good to be true!' Nan expertly dunked the rest of her biscuit in the tea and into her mouth before continuing. 'And the younger one, what's she called, Reagan?'

'It's Kennedy, Nan.'

'Daft calling your child after an assassinated American president. Asking for trouble is that.'

I knew what was coming next. I started to giggle in anticipation.

'She nearly killed you once. If I hadn't come into the room you'd have choked to death.'

'She was only a baby too and she was trying to be nice by feeding me sweets.'

'The ones who try to kill you with kindness are the worst.' Nan harrumphed as she speed-read one of the brochures. 'You've got more sense, Ava. How's school?'

For me that is like someone asking how I'm feeling after having all my fingernails torn off. I pulled a face. 'Miss Duncan thinks I'll be able to do well in A-level textiles. There are some other practical courses I can take.'

'That's champion, Ava! About time that fancy school did something useful for you instead of pinning all those daft labels on you. How's your father?'

'Dad's the same as ever. He works too hard.'

Nan nodded. 'It's a demanding job putting the world to rights. Sometimes it means that you can't see the wood for the trees.'

Mum came in from the kitchen and waved her yellow rubber-gloved hands at us. 'What have you two been talking about?' she asked.

'Trees and wood,' I said.

Nan's voice sounded sharper. 'Ava has been waving these flashy brochures in front of my nose. I may not be as clever as you but I've learned that you can't gloss over old age, Elspeth.'

'I knew you'd take it the wrong way.' Mum sighed and

snapped off a rubber glove. 'As you would put it, Mum, "I can't do right for doing wrong".'

They glared at each other for a while. I scuttled off to top up the teapot.

After that, Nan dozed off in her chair whilst Mum vacuumed the stairs. It was amazing watching Mum clean. She never cleaned at home as we had Irene, our housekeeper, plus a cleaner who came in three mornings a week. I was left sitting next to Nan watching a TV programme about buying holiday villas in Bulgaria. Every so often Nan would wake up and pass comment.

I decided that now would be a good time to take my overnight bag up to Mum's old bedroom. It was cooler up there.

It was hard to imagine Mum living in that room when she was my age and she never spoke about what it was like. She was not one of those rags to riches people who are always banging on about the hard times and how it made them who they are today. Nor was she a pretender denying her roots. She just never spoke about it, which meant that you had to go hunting for clues.

On top of the bookcase was a black and white old primary school class photo. There in the front row, Mum glared out at me from the past with her hair tamed in tight braids and wearing thick glasses.

'You got them free on the National Health,' Nan had told me. Mum still kept them in a drawer in the house.

Her *memento mori* she called them and would sometimes get them out to illustrate some humiliating point at dinner parties.

'Ava, I'm off now,' Mum called up the stairs.

I joined them in the hall as Nan handed her a package wrapped in tin foil.

'I've made you a bacon sandwich. You never know what sort of food they'll be dishing up at these conferences.'

They both smiled.

Families are weird, aren't they? Mum and Nan had this food code that they used instead of saying sorry. They always made sure that as they were leaving one of them handed the other a gift of food.

Vix

Ambition is often raw
Like exposed flesh
Hard to look at
But even harder to stop
Wanting to look at
My latest assignment comes back
Only sixty-eight per cent
Not good enough, not nearly good enough for me
Only sixty-eight per cent
That won't get me the grade that
I need
It feels like someone has slapped
Cold water on my face
The teacher
Must have made a mistake
I tried really hard
Do I have to beg and plead?
Turn a little nasty to get the grade I need?
That night
It starts

I take up nail scissors
And
Make my first mark
It is ninety per cent successful
Funny how at the time
You don't feel the sting
Only the tingle
Of doing a forbidden thing
And the relief of being
Out of yourself for a while
Brain churning
Hot but never burning
Like clothes in a tumble dryer
It's not like a dream
But it is unreal
And familiar
Like reading about celebrities in a magazine

Ava

Nan and I spent the rest of the afternoon in her small kitchen making a cheese and onion pie together. First of all she made me run my fingers under the tap.

'You need cold hands for making pastry.'

As we were rolling out the pastry, she waggled the rolling pin at me, saying, 'I'm not totally useless, am I?'

'Nan, it's not like that. When we got the phone call two days ago we were all really worried.'

'It was only a false alarm. You've no need to worry. I've been going to a day centre. You get a hot meal and there're activities laid on like art and bingo. I particularly like the art. I've been doing my life story in papier mâché.'

'What!'

'Sounds ridiculous, but ripping up paper and shaping a landscape of memories really got me thinking about the things that made my life worthwhile.'

'Life as layers of experience piled on top of each other,' I said as I sprinkled the cheese on the onions. Nan added the top crust and we took turns at putting the thumb marks around the side.

Nan pinched the side of my cheek leaving a floury smudge.

Later on, as I was nodding off in front of the gas fire, trying to imagine what landscape my life story would look like – probably lonely and bleak like the surface of Mars – Nan asked, 'Have you brought any of your dolls to show me?'

I shyly rustled something in the carrier bag at the edge of my chair. I had left it there earlier.

'Come on, don't be shy.'

The rest of the family thought my Bootsale Barbies were a huge joke but Nan had always loved them.

'All great crafts people learn their trade by making miniatures,' she'd say.

I unwrapped the doll. 'It's a 1960s cocktail dress. The net underskirt was really hard to get right. It's early 1960s, before the mini-skirt took off.' I lifted it out of the bag and handed it and the old pattern over.

Nan chuckled. 'That short skirt got the blame for all the ills in the world.' She put on her reading glasses and scrutinised the doll as I babbled on.

'I got the fabric from an Oxfam shop. It took me ages to track it down. I'm still not sure about the colour.'

'I had one just like that myself. Went dancing every weekend before I fell pregnant with your mother. Used to have to spray the skirts with starch to get them to stick up. I think I have a can in the cupboard under the

66

sink.' She jumped up from the chair but then stopped in her tracks and clutched her side.

'What it is, Nan?'

She waved me away with her hand. 'Just got up too quick, that's all. What am I like? Keep forgetting I'm seventy-odd and not seventeen.'

I made us another pot of tea and Nan deliberately put her cup down on top of the retirement home magazines.

'How is Elspeth? Working too hard I suppose?'

I nodded. 'Mum never stops. There have even been suggestions that she'll be a judge in a few years' time.'

'It must be hard for you living in a family of brain-boxes.'

'I've got my job in the café to keep me sane,' I said, grinning back.

'The one with the daft name.'

'The Cakewalk is a fashion-themed café. Tasha is a fantastic boss. We have a laugh.'

Nan leaned over and grabbed my wrist and squeezed it hard. 'Ava, don't you let them crush your spirit. I know a thing or two about feeling like an outsider.' Her eyes had a fierce tinge to them. Then she sat back in her armchair and sighed. 'It wasn't easy being a single parent in the 1960s, you know. Unmarried mothers we were called in them days and people looked down their noses at us. And I was the lowest of the low because I had a half-caste baby.'

'We don't use terms like that now, Nan. It's offensive.'
I sighed.

'Aye, but don't forget that's what they used to say and much worse and your mam had to take it. That's what's made her so tough and successful.'

Mum never let anyone off the hook. I thought about that face glaring out at the world in the class photo.

'I am proud of Elspeth and I probably don't let her know it enough. It's just the way I was brought up. Girls weren't supposed to get above themselves and too much praise was akin to spoiling a child. If I had my time again, I'd do things a bit differently. Put less pressure on her to always be the best.'

She sat back in the chair and closed her eyes.

'Nan, do you ever think that your life might have been easier if you hadn't gone to that dance and . . .'

'Meeting Elspeth's father was one of the high points of my life. Victor was wonderful and Elspeth takes after him. He was studying law on a scholarship that he had sweated blood to get. He was a very proud man and always so smartly dressed and polite. The dance wasn't the only time I met him. We saw a lot of each other for the best part of a year. I always knew more than I let on to Elspeth.'

'Why did you never say anything?' I asked after a shocked silence.

'It was complicated. I knew that Victor was in danger when he went back home. His country had only just been granted its independence and there was all sorts of jostling for power and political intrigue. I didn't know all the ins and outs of it, but I knew that if he didn't come back . . . well, it meant that he wasn't able to. I didn't want to add to his worries by telling him about the baby. If he could come back, there would be a lovely surprise waiting for him.'

'But why didn't you tell Mum?'

'People didn't talk so openly then and the thinking was "least said, soonest mended". I didn't want to go raising her hopes and mine. When it was clear that he wasn't coming back, I just put him to the back of my mind and got on with the job of earning a living for the both of us and seeing that Elspeth didn't go short of anything. I was hard on her because I knew she'd face prejudice and meanness. Not knowing about her father would give her one less thing to worry about. More than anything you want to spare your children from pain. Besides, I knew that he loved me and I loved him.'

She pulled out a crumpled tissue from up her sleeve and blew her nose loudly.

I got up out of the chair and sat down at her feet, dropping my head into her lap and she stroked my head.

'You remind me of him,' she said. 'Elspeth and Victoria may have inherited his head for facts but you've got his sparkle. Victor could light up a room. I think they call it charisma.'

'I don't feel very sparkly.'

Nan tugged firmly at one of my curls.

'OW!'

'You will sparkle, Ava, believe me you will. One day you will come into your own.'

I really wanted to believe her, even if I wasn't totally sure what coming into your own meant. I assumed it was something like feeling comfortable in your own skin. Coming to a point where the inner and outer you are perfectly balanced and no one can make you feel inferior without your consent.

Vix

I panicked when I saw the mark
Now my feelings show
And people can ask questions
If I don't come up with
A damn good
Explanation
Plaster over the cracks
Rework the essay
Have to try harder
To make it look easy
Give myself a thrown-together look
That works
Primark dress with shoes from Prada
But I'll never do that again
Never

Rosamund got eighty-eight per cent
'Shitty mark,' she sighed. 'I need to be in the
      nineties.'
She took out her lip-gloss

'I hate it when things don't go well.
Let's go to Salvador's.'
I don't really feel like drinking
But Rosamund orders
Two shady ladies
'Drinking stops me thinking
And feeling for a while,'
She says with a knowing smile
Because it feels like
She can look inside
And see the need in me
To make a mark

Ava

The next morning Nan woke me up at some ridiculous hour. She placed a strong mug of sweet tea on the bedside table. 'We're going on a magical mystery tour.'

'Nan, it's seven a.m.' Then I wondered if she should be going out so soon after coming out of hospital. 'Where are we going, then?' I asked.

'It wouldn't be a mystery if I told you, but here's a clue: we're catching the bus to the city centre.'

The bus was crowded and airless but Nan didn't seem to mind as much as I did. First stop was a market where we stocked up on half-price bacon and spent ages stroking bales of fabric on another stall as Nan tried to show me how to tell the thread count of cotton by its touch.

After a short tea break we caught another bus up to the university. Then we meandered around some streets while Nan tried to get her bearings. Eventually we ended up in a side street.

'This is where I used to work. It was the law faculty then. It's too small nowadays for the number of students.

This is where I met Victor.' Then she opened up her handbag.

'This is a photo of him. I've never shown anyone this before.'

She held out a small square piece of paper. A tiny black and white photo with a white border. Nan held it tightly in her hand and pointed to one of the group of shy-looking men that were standing outside this building.

'That's him.'

It was weird looking at the photo of him. A total stranger and yet my grandfather. Stranger and relative.

'You've got his eyes,' Nan said, and then she scooped up the picture and made a sort of whooping sound.

'Are you OK?'

'You don't know how long I've been waiting to say that. It makes me feel bold, like I could achieve anything.'

She linked her arm in mine and we walked inside. The building had been converted into an administration block for the university.

The receptionist, who was wearing a purple synthetic uniform with a plastic name badge that said *Marilyn*, looked up at our arrival and frowned.

Nan began speaking. 'I used to work here in the 1960s. I was wondering if I could just show my granddaughter, who is up from London, the main hall. It was where I met her grandfather.'

My face was burning with embarrassment but the

receptionist smiled and said, 'I don't see why not but don't be too long as we have a meeting soon in there.'

It was an oak-panelled room with lots of paintings and a wooden floor but it had modern furnishings. Stainless steel and chrome chairs and futuristic tables.

I thought Nan would be upset but she smiled.

'Life moves on.'

A young man in a matching purple uniform appeared with a sleek black tray with a white china pot and two cups. 'Marilyn said you might like some tea.' He placed the tray on a table and left us.

'Do you miss him?'

Nan sipped her tea. 'I miss the idea of him. I miss the warmth of being loved and touched by a man who loves you.'

I felt my face going hot for the second time that day.

'We went to the law society ball which was held in here. What a night that was. I wore a turquoise satin cocktail dress – similar in style to the one you made for your doll. The trouble I had getting gloves to match! Spent a fortune on them. Victor bought me some gardenias. Have you ever smelled a gardenia?'

I shook my head.

'They smell like expensive French perfume.'

'This all makes me feel so sad,' I said as I looked around the room. 'That you had so little time together.'

'I look at Elspeth and you and Victoria and the feeling

of pride that I have in you stamps out all the sadness. A layer of pride papers over the pain.'

'But wouldn't you like to have seen him one more time? To let him know about Mum?'

'If I'd been living in a storybook then I could've answered his letter, but I was in the real world. Like I said yesterday, I was an unmarried mother and I needed to have my parents' support if I was going to keep Elspeth.' Nan's voice sounded as hard and scratchy as sandpaper.

'Did they want you to get rid of Mum?'

'They weren't bad people. They were frightened about what would become of me. They wanted me to put her up for adoption and I thought about it, and when they realised that Victor was African that was another bombshell. The arguments it caused . . . In the end it was my father that decided. "That child is a Broadhurst and we will not abandon a Broadhurst." His only condition was that I was to have nothing to do with Victor. What did I care at that time? I was never going to hear from him again, was I?'

'And did you?' Hadn't Nan said something about a letter?

Nan stood up. 'It's time we were getting home. Your mother will be back to pick you up in a couple of hours.'

We got a taxi back as Nan looked worn out. We watched TV together until we heard Mum's car pull up outside the house and I went upstairs to get my overnight bag. Nan met me on the landing. She was holding a battered old shoebox.

'I've sorted you out some of my old patterns and silk threads.' Then she kissed me on the cheek and whispered, 'I'll speak to Elspeth about Victor myself. It'll be better coming from me. Promise me you won't say anything until the time is right. You mustn't breathe a word of this to anyone. It would cause no end of trouble if you did.'

I nodded and we kissed goodbye.

As Mum and I were getting in the car, Nan winked at me and she thrust one of the retirement home brochures through the window. 'This one looks bearable – if you're sure you can afford it.'

Mum smiled. 'We'll see you on Christmas Day.'

That would give me time to find out more about Victor.

But five days later she was dead.

So when would the time be right?

Vix

Christmas in the Caribbean
Is supposed to cheer us up
Dad works
Mum cries and rages
I shirk and Ava lies
Under a palm tree
Her busy fingers weaving leaves
Now that Nan has gone
The pressure's on
Because life is over before it has begun
Rosamund sends me texts and jpegs
Of the wild party that I missed –
Or when Pascal asked
Where I was
Without u it's crap
We commiserate
I walk along the beach
Paddling idly along the shore until
Sharp seashell cuts into my foot
A young local girl and her mother

Cut some aloe vera
And pour on the clear jelly as
I watch
Detached from my body
It feels good
To part company from myself
Again
To be simply
A thing to be healed

Ava

After the Christmas holidays were over, I worked extra shifts at the café and spent all my free time wandering the galleries of the Victoria and Albert Museum. Feeling invisible in the crowds and looking at beautiful things made me feel better. Occasionally I bumped into Miss Duncan and we would sigh over an early Vivienne Westwood or an Ossie Clark dress but the excitement would soon pass. Without Nan, everything I did, said or thought felt wrong. Inside I was numb. Snooping was the only thing that made me tingle with life. Even the shameful feelings that came afterwards were better than feeling nothing or the constant playing over in my mind of the last day we spent together.

I had found out that our housekeeper, Irene, plays online poker when she's supposed to be ordering the groceries and that Jonathon dabs my mother's *Crème de la Mer* on his spots.

You can't really snoop on Tasha because everything is laid bare for you anyway. It is the opposite with her. She tells you too much information.

I also discovered that my parents had lied about when they got married and, by adding an extra year, they had covered up the fact that Mum had been pregnant with Vix. Was that why Dad stayed with her and ended it with Catherine?

I still went into Dad's office but his PC was always shut down and I couldn't find his password.

I was finding it hard to sleep and would often get up in the night to make myself a hot chocolate.

One night I could hear voices as I made my way down the stairs. Mum and Dad were still in the kitchen. I froze on the stairs and listened.

Mum said, 'Sometimes I think you are sorry that she married God instead of you.'

'She wouldn't have had a chance once I'd seen you in action at the debating society.' Dad was moving into smooth mode and I was thinking it was time I wasn't there. No one likes to hang around when their parents are getting soppy with each other.

Then Dad changed the subject. 'Maybe it's time to start facing up to your past, Elspeth. Try and make contact with your father. I could make some discreet enquiries at the Foreign Office. There will be visa documentation about who was in the country at that time. We know that he was studying law so that should narrow it down. It's a long shot but it's worth a try.'

Mum's voice rose. 'Alan, please respect my feelings

and don't allude to my so-called father again. The last thing I want is anyone meddling in my business. The past is another country that I have no desire to visit.'

I tiptoed back to my room. There was no way I was going to tell her what Nan had told me now.

Vix and I hardly saw each other. She was always with Rosamund and if they weren't revising they were out partying or having one of their private conversations.

Kennedy was still popping into the café every Saturday where she would demolish cake and talk at me about what a wonderful time she was having. Or she would bring in a flyer about a church bazaar or jumble sale. I have to admit that she was pretty good at getting herself and Precious between a rival bargain hunter and a prize object.

Pascal ordered his birthday cake from us and Tasha insisted that I have a go at designing it, so Tasha and I went over and I drew some quick sketches. Then we spent ages after work experimenting with sponge, silver food colouring and marzipan trying to get the shape of the bar right. It was long and narrow and chrome. Most of our creations ended up looking like an explosion in a scrapyard but we did laugh a lot.

Miss Duncan suggested that I make up a fabric version of the cake as well, like the artist Claes Oldenburg, for my portfolio. She showed me a book of his giant slices of cake or giant soft plug sockets. They were very funny and they did make you look at everyday things in a different way.

She also handed out scraps of paper and asked us all to write down our ideas for our work experience placement.

It took me ages to think about it. There is something scary about putting your dreams down on paper. At first I wrote, *Work in fabric section of a store* – but then just as we were handing them in I scrubbed that out and wrote, *Costume part of Victoria and Albert Museum*. I didn't tell anyone else about it partly because I was afraid they'd laugh at me, partly because they might steal my idea. Some things are too important to talk about.

Vix

I spent four hours getting ready
Tweezing even the stray hairs on my toes
Constantly changing my clothes
Rosamund texted me five times
Winding me up about how she just knew
That Pascal was *only interested in being with u*
It was like a game of verbal snap
He likes you
No, no he likes you,
Me, you, me
Snap
I don't even like Pascal that much
OK his parents are stinking rich
And that gives him a confidence that's cool
He knows loads of people, he owns Salvador's
Runs the club
Garage, soul, 80s pop with some lounge
    thrown in for when things get too much
What would Pascal see in a gal like me?
Rosamund and I like to arrive late

The wine bar's full

There are a few girls from school and some older
friends

We order some cocktails

And so the night begins and

I pretend that I'm having fun

Everything has to be big in a club

Overstretched smiles, loud laughs, touching and
feeling

I kiss Pascal a few times (it's his birthday)

He smokes too much and his aftershave marks my
skin

Like a greasy stain

Rosamund disappears for a while

Pascal is at the turntables and in this noisy
pushing shoving space

I feel alone

I stand and sip my drink looking quickly
round

Not wanting to catch anyone's eye

I turn round too fast and accidentally jolt an
elbow

'Sorry,' we both say together and I smile

The drink wobbles and settles in the glass

The boy

Looks at me

He dresses like an R&B star

Baggy and expensive
And his aftershave is light and blends with his
        sweat
He is part of the South London Crew that Pascal
        invites to add an 'edge' to his club night
We don't say much but he doesn't move away and
        neither do I
We focus on the music
Or elbows' touch
'People call me Ice. You live around here?'
I nod
'What's your name?'
'I'm Vix.' My voice raises above the music
A wisp of hair mingled with sweat and smoky
        club smells gets in the way
He pulls it away. I sip on my drink but can't seem
        to swallow
'Unusual name.'
I flounder – should I babble on that my real name is
        Victoria but my friends have shortened it
Or shall I give him my second version – the one
        Rosamund and I made up?
'I'm Vixen – that's a female fox.'
His friends come up and laugh
'Sounds like someone who takes part in wrestling
        on my Xbox.'
Lucky for me they all move along

Cos I'm feeling tacky and I've got it all wrong
I find Rosamund and some others from school
I drink more cocktails and try and act cool
We take the dance floor by storm
Pascal tries to kiss me again but this time I'm not
sure
Keep watching that boy and feel he's scoping me
too
By the bar we meet again but his friends stick like
superglue
The club night finishes and we all spill out
I have to eat a kebab – what's that all about?
We screech into the shop and then lurch into the
street
Kebab and alcohol not the best cocktail mix
As we walk to the taxi stand I start to feel sick
Pascal doesn't want us messing up his car
The effort I have to make to maintain my dignity
And when I give in and let it all out
The vomit is projectile
As I'm coming up for breath
I come face to face with
The guardian of appropriateness
The legendary
Mrs Berry
As she sails past
Eyes aghast

Cosseted in her Nissan Cherry

Shame tastes sour
But I am past caring
I find a FemFresh in my bag
And wipe my face
Realise that the others have
Flagged down a cab
But I'm not alone
Pascal says
'Come on, Vixen,
I'll walk you home.'

I have had too much
Alcohol
And I smell of sick
So am not at my best
We hover outside for a while
'I'll be OK now.'
He doesn't move
Suddenly I find my
Inner Hildegard
My own cold front
Because I don't know
Where I am
With Pascal
I don't know what to do

He nods and we go inside
I must clean my teeth
And wipe my face
So I pour him a glass of water
Point out the downstairs loo
And try and gather
Myself
Run upstairs, brush my teeth
Splash my face
And spray on
Some of my mother's Youth Dew
We sit in the sitting room
He inspects the room
Admires the type of brandy
Which I pour him
Close to him on the sofa now
Can feel his breathing
He talks about Ava
How he thinks she's really
Clever
He goes to the bathroom and then
Walks out the door
Says goodbye
No pretend affection
Just an out and out
Rejection

Ava

I couldn't bring myself to open Nan's shoebox until close to the end of March. As the days were lighter and daffodils brightened the parks and window boxes, I dug it out from under the bed and left it on the floor in the middle of my room for a few days. On my third attempt at opening it, I was able to reach my hand in and touch the objects. The box had the familiar musty smell of Nan's house.

Amongst the fabric scraps, tangles of embroidery thread and packets of needles were five dress patterns. The packets were tatty with use with scraps of fabric and thread stuffed in them. There was a flowery summer dress, a trouser suit, a beach robe and turban and a knitting pattern for matching Arran jumpers for a whole family. Inside that pattern was a photo of Vix and me wearing the jumpers, or rather the jumpers wearing us. Only one packet lay smooth and untouched. It was a pattern for a 'modern, elegant, knee-length wedding dress'. The swatches of fabric that Nan had chosen were pale lemon.

Nan must have been so happy when she bought this

wedding dress pattern, I thought as I opened the packet.

Alongside the thin tissue paper pattern and samples of fabric that were stuffed inside was a letter. I didn't notice it at first because it was an incredibly neat and small pale blue envelope.

My lonely room

Dear Jean,

I have just dropped you off at your digs and decided to save the bus fare and walk home. If truth be told, I needed the fresh air. You looked so lovely this evening – like a flower in your summer dress. I'm chuckling to myself because I can hear your voice saying, 'Give over, Victor' or feel you digging me in the ribs and with a 'Less of your flannel!' Sometimes I wish that you would accept compliments a little more graciously but I will just have to keep showering them on you until you get the message and believe that you truly are a very special person.

I realised that the first time I saw you in the canteen. I had been having a pretty miserable time of it. England is a wonderful country, but everything is so grey and narrow and slightly grubby and I'd had huge expectations about coming. Nothing short of having tea with the Queen would do for

me. It was a shock to find out that England was not
so delighted to receive a darkie like me.

You always had a smile for me and not one of
those 'Let's be nice to our poor foreign chums' types
– a real smile. And you remembered how much I
liked rice pudding and kept a bowlful back for me if
I had a late lecture. There are so many wonderful
things about you. How do I love thee? Let me count
the ways!

The way you are so proud of where you come
from and speak about Manchester. The way you
appreciate a good piece of cloth (my mother would
be impressed). The way that you read good books
for pleasure. How you recklessly kissed me in the
cinema.

You have so many qualities.

I am so honoured that you have agreed to come
to the law society ball with me next week.

Yours fervently,
Victor

'And I am so proud of you too, Nan,' I whispered. I tried
to fold the letter back into its envelope but my hand
shook. If only there had been more time to talk to Nan
about her life. There were so many scenes that I wanted
to share with her. I – or rather an older and wiser version
of myself – wanted to sit her down and tell her not to be

so hard on herself and that she had done the best for Mum and for us by just being herself. That by loving Victor she had played a part in creating us. Then I would tell her all my hopes and dreams and she would say, 'That's champion, Ava.'

I decided that I would make her outfits in miniature – the flowery dress, the trouser suit, the beach robe, even the knitted family. I would make a separate landscape for each of them too. It would be like recreating those happy times in her life and I could feel close to her again.

Except for the wedding dress. I didn't have the heart to make that one.

Vix

The devil makes work for idle hands
Is the theme of Monday assembly
So when the A-level students have finished their
Revision
What about using their free time
To relax and smooth the pre-exam frown
By designing and creating a fabulous ballgown for
        the end of term prom
Purely voluntarily
The thought of this makes me feel sick again
But I go along with it and smile and say
What a great decision

Ava

Only a school that boasted a one hundred per cent success rate in its A-levels would dare to put on a prom party on the very day in August when the results came out. Supreme self-confidence is what some people call it. Extreme arrogance is how it feels to me.

School ends in July, but all the girls who had just left always came back for the Hildegard prom party in August – even if it meant chartering your own private jet to get you back from your island hideaway in time to collect your results and go to the party. The senior boys from the local boys' private school provided partners.

Not only did you have to take and pass so many A-levels but now you were also expected to design your own gown for the prom party. At Hildegard you were expected to be super talented at everything.

I blinked. This was a unique moment. Vix had texted me saying she would come to my room in five minutes, just like old times. My head swam with all these cosy fantasies about girlie chats and I even thought that now would be a good time to talk to someone about Nan or how I'd screwed up with that e-mail and letter from Catherine. It was still in my sewing basket ticking away like a time bomb. At least I had not read it. I took out a box of pins and closed the lid quickly. Some of the pins dropped like silver ash onto the floor. I patted the carpet to find them and carried on with the miniature summer dress of Nan's.

A couple of minutes later Vix walked in smelling of expensive bath products and, even though it was just ten o'clock, she was wearing pyjamas. She took a deep breath and said quickly, 'We have to design an evening gown for the prom party and I really haven't got the time with all my revision and stuff. Will you help me?'

For once I had something that Vix wanted. It might actually be fun to spend some time together like we used to. There was a lot I could teach her. Vix continued, 'You will follow my instructions and, of course, I will pay you if that's what's bothering you.' She frowned at me.

Was her opinion of me really that low? I shook my head and replied, 'I can't help you. I've got some course-work to finish off.' I paused. If I wanted to have a meaningful talk with my sister then maybe I should be the one to start it off. If her opinion of me was really that low then I had to change it.

'My work experience placement'll take up a lot of my time. I'm really hoping to get the Victoria and Albert Museum. I think I'm in with a chance,' I told her, sharing my news with someone other than Miss Duncan.

Vix's expression hardened and her lips tightened. 'I see. Your work experience placement means that you can't help me,' she said through gritted teeth. And before I could say anything else she was storming towards the door. Vix was used to getting her own way. Who knows what she'd be capable of?

I was just about to stop her and tell her that of course I'd help her with the dress when she screamed, 'What's that?'

The way she looked at me you'd think I'd deliberately jabbed that pin under her foot.

Vix

Time passes
See a pin, pick it up
All the day you'll have . . .
Sweet thoughts to suck on
As you imagine it
Pick, pick, picking away
At a corner of your skin
Pin on skin
No need to think
No time to be afraid
Pin on skin
Waiting for my life to begin
Two days before I sit my exams

Time passes
Too late
For revision plans
Handy tips and last minute crams
Good luck card
Makes me feel

Soft instead of hard
So tonight
Take a long lavender bath
Wash hair
Massage nails with cream to make them grow
Eat a square of organic chocolate
Try taking three deep breaths
Saying
This is not happening to me
Not really happening to me
Screw my eyes in the mirror
To distort image
Then take a peep
Still me
Light a candle
It has to be
My cool hard lover
My dashing blade
Who strokes my skin
Who breaks the ice
Makes me feel soft and nice
Before
My exams will start to bite
Tomorrow

Ava

During A-level exam week, Hildegard takes on the atmosphere of a nunnery. There are signs everywhere warning you to be quiet because an exam is taking place behind a door. Pale-faced girls whisper into mobile phones in the playground like they are seeking confession.

At the end of my lesson, Miss Duncan came and sat beside me.

'Sorry I haven't had much time to check on your work. I've been inundated with requests for advice on making dresses for the prom party. I suggested that they go to an expert,' Miss Duncan explained.

'Mum would pay any consultant a hefty fee for the best advice,' I replied.

'*You* are the expert, silly,' Miss Duncan said. 'Have a bit of faith in yourself.'

'I think hell would freeze over before Vix asked me for help again.' I told Miss Duncan that I'd already told Vix I'd be too busy to help. 'She wasn't too pleased. She and Rosamund have been planning the party at Salvador's for ever.'

Miss Duncan laughed. 'We were all amazed when Mrs Berry agreed to have the party there.'

'Rosamund and my sister can be a force to be reckoned with.'

'They must have got her on a good day. Either that or her agreeing to it was part of her business in partnership with the school programme. It might be worth reconsidering because it would be a good thing to have in your portfolio.' Miss Duncan opened a file and continued, 'I've put your name forward for the placement that you wanted.'

'Oh!'

She smiled back at me. It was good to know that somebody had faith in me.

Vix

The exams are over
So
Rosamund and I spend Saturdays
Together
So we can shop
And have a manicure or facial
Plan for the prom party
Talk as we torment a small amount of food
On a large white china plate
With a fork
In an exclusive restaurant

That day she leaned over
The table
And said
'I like you Vix, because you
See things the way that I do.'
She hands me a small black case
Inside it is lined with velvet
And holds a small jewelled knife

She gently rolls up her
Sleeve to show me
Her marks
'You are a soul mate
Comprendez?'
'How did you know?'
I ask
'I sensed it at first
The smell of kindred spirit
And then I saw the mark
On your leg
And a fine dot of blood on your shirt.
Then little things
Gave you away
No short sleeves
The way you drive yourself
With no reprieve
People won't get it
But I do
No one will understand you
Like I do.
Together we can help
Each other through.'
My throat is dry so
I nod and
We click on our pedometers
And walk

Arms linked
Pockets lined with
Matching secrets
Queens of the King's Road

Ava

Irene was cleaning the cooker and I was eating my breakfast when Mum appeared from the garden after her Early Bird gym session. She frowned at me. 'Ava, is chocolate spread really the most nutritious option?'

'It settles my stomach,' I replied. One day soon she'll realise that no amount of gluten free products or fish oil capsules will turn me into a genius. I didn't say anything more, because today was officially my last day of school before my three-week work placement which would be announced today.

Jonathon rode up the gravel on his bike. He winked at me through the window and walked into the kitchen. As he was undoing his helmet strap, Mum said, 'Family dinner tonight, Jonathon. Could you pick up a few things from the deli?'

'Sure,' he said as he sent a text to Vix. She never emerged until the very last moment saying, 'I don't do people in the mornings!'

He took the car keys, but Mum said, 'Don't use the four-by-four this week. Alan has been tipped off that you might get papped dropping the girls off at school. There is going to be a big demonstration outside the school about Chelsea tractors. Alan is working on an air pollution bill at the moment so it wouldn't go down well. Take Victoria's Mini Cooper.'

'I don't see why I can't drive myself to school.' Vix appeared at the front door dressed in a Prada sundress, long-sleeved cardigan, big sunglasses and perfectly groomed hair. 'I've taken my A-levels and if I wasn't organising the prom party I wouldn't be going at all.' She sighed as she pulled out a notebook from her latest Mulberry handbag.

'I refuse to pay any more of your parking fines,' Mum replied. 'Jonathon has to pick up some shopping so it's more practical for him to drive.' Mum continued. 'I would like us all to sit together round a table and share a meal and have a conversation this evening.'

Vix looked bored and said, 'So we have to change our plans to assuage your liberal upper-middle-class guilt.'

'That's right! Now get yourself off to that expensive school paid for out of the money I have wrung from the fat cats and captains of industry!'

They both grinned. Jonathon shook the car keys and we went outside.

Vix sighed. 'I hope you aren't wearing that aftershave again. Made my car stink last time you used it.'

Jonathon opened the car door. 'Today, ladies, the

cologne I am wearing is a select blend of lime, basil, cinnamon and musk specifically designed to be irresistible to the discerning nose.'

Vix's response was to light a cigarette.

'Your parents don't approve of smoking and neither do I,' Jonathon said as we left.

'As my mother's law firm has represented the tobacco industry in the past she is in no position to pass judgement on me.' She blew smoke rings around the car.

'You'll get Jonathon sacked and if Mrs Berry smells smoke on me I'll have to tell her in order not to incriminate myself,' I told her.

'Drop me off at the Cakewalk then. I'm meeting Rosamund, Kennedy and their mother there,' she snapped at us. Her parting shot as she slammed the car door a short while later was, 'You're like a couple of old women.'

We sat in silence for a while before Jonathon said, 'I could've handled that better.'

'The smoking-gives-you-early-onset-wrinkles line might have been a better tactic,' I suggested.

Jonathon thumped the steering wheel, 'Now you tell me!'

'Sorry, I've only just thought of it.'

'Someone didn't take their fish oil capsules this morning! I thought you were looking a bit queasy over breakfast.'

We both laughed. Jonathon never made me feel stupid.

He put on a ham American accent as we drove to school and asked, 'So tell me, what are you trying to hide? I can read you like a book.'

'Jonathon, you must promise not to tell a soul . . .' I had to speak about this to someone.

He quickly crossed his heart, licked his little finger and smoothed each eyebrow before saying, 'I do.'

I took a launch pad of a breath. 'Dad used to be in love with an old friend from university.'

Jonathon's mouth dropped open.

'A woman called Sister Catherine.'

'In love with a nun!' Jonathon gasped. 'It's like *The Thorn Birds* all over again.'

'What are you talking about?' I was beginning to regret telling him already.

'Ignore me. It's a cult TV classic about a woman who falls in love with a priest.'

'Catherine wasn't a nun then! This happened when they were at university together.'

Jonathon turned to look at me. 'Have you been up to your old tricks again, my little snoop doggie snoop?'

'I spotted an old video tape marked *Graduation* and I thought it would be fun to see Dad in his cap and gown and ridiculous 1980s hairdo so I watched it. Only there was something else on the tape . . . Won't we be late for school?'

'I'll drive you right up to the front gate. Go on.'

'It was a tape of Dad and Katy, as she was called before she became Sister Catherine. They were filming each other on some walk in the country but they looked so happy to be together and they swear that they love each other. Just lately they have begun e-mailing each other. Don't ask me how I know.' I stopped. 'You won't tell anyone, will you? Only I had to tell someone; it was bothering me so much.'

'My lips are sealed. Busy Mates are the souls of discretion.'

I got out of the car and raced towards the textiles room. It felt good to have told somebody.

Vix

Rosamund's mother
Has a friend
Who lives on only light
No food, no water
Nothing in the fridge
Just light

Flicking through the pages of her magazine
Kennedy started to complain
'Mrs Berry didn't feel that working in TopShop
        was an experience.'
I said, 'Ava is going to the V&A.'
Kennedy sat up,
'I could do that.'
Rosamund's mum smiled
'V&A
Has a certain cachet.'
All I cared about was
If Rosamund and I had to live
On rays of light

She'd survive on less than me
Be better than me
More competitive

Ava

The first thing that greeted me when I walked through the door that morning was a hideous poster advertising the prom party.

CELEBRATE YOUR A's IN STYLE
AT SALVADOR'S

COMPLIMENTARY
CHAMPAGNE COCKTAIL

TICKETS AVAILABLE FROM
SIXTH FORM COMMON ROOM

The school leavers had whipped themselves up into a frenzy because this year the party was going to be held at Salvador's.

I was making my way towards Miss Duncan's office when I heard voices.

'I just try and match the person to the placement that I think they'll get most benefit from.'

'And you're doing a marvellous job.' Mrs Berry overemphasised the word marvellous making it sound exactly the opposite.

I held my breath. I could sense a 'but' coming. 'We're not being funny but are you and Victoria really sisters? I mean, she is so clever' being one of my all-time favourites. Mrs Berry's 'but' was a real cracker.

'But the V&A is a very prestigious placement and we do have the reputation of the school to consider.'

There was a pause before Miss Duncan responded. 'Ava is very accomplished.'

'At needlework, yes, but the reputation of Hildegard School is one of high academic achievement combined with practical excellence. Her grandmother's death has affected her a lot. So all things considered it would be infinitely more appropriate for Kennedy to take up the placement.'

Miss Duncan sighed. 'I have already mentioned it and she was really excited at the prospect.'

'I'm sure a woman of your flair and resourcefulness can think of some other placement for her.'

Another placement for the stupid Other, I thought.

When I came back twenty minutes later, the best excuse that she had come up with was, 'I'm really sorry, but I'm afraid there's been some sort of mix up. I know you like your job at the Cakewalk and it is a fashion café so you could do a placement there. I'll arrange it.'

I nodded and mumbled something and I did the only thing I could think of.

I retraced my steps and walked right out of school.

My stomach bloated with rage. I knew who was to blame for this – the only other person who knew about the placement. Vix.

Vix

In Rosamund's room
There are pale apricot roses
And a chest of drawers made from glass
She closes the curtains and we take two giant-
    sized cushions and sit on the floor
There is no need to speak
The ritual is deeper than words
We close our eyes
And I feel the weight of all my failures and
    ugliness and imperfection
I let the feeling rise in me
I release the stone in my stomach that has been
    weighing them down
The feelings rise up and flow freely through my
    body
Then we take out our cases and open them
    together
We each reach out
Rosamund nods at me if I hesitate or draw in my
    breath

'Release the pain'
'Feel perfect'
We hold our blades up to the light
Run them up and down the skin on our arms
The fine hairs stand on end
Feelings have blown up like an air bag inside me
Pushing me outside of myself
I am floating on a cushion of marshmallows
Too sweet – too sweet but I can't stop
Even though I know the sweetness will hurt later
And that the disgust doubles and thickens each
    time
For the moment it is enough
Everything changes shape
We make one pure cut each
I can't help noticing that
Rosamund's is more perfect than mine
And even though the rule is
One cut
She had started another one

Ava

Irene was in the kitchen chopping some vegetables. 'Why you back early?' she said, keeping her back to me.

'Things to do,' I muttered. 'I've got issues.'

'You got cold or something? Stay away from me, I don't want it.'

What had I come home for? I was feeling angry, hurt and, for some reason that I didn't understand, ashamed. Why was I so pathetic and powerless? Tears welled up inside of me and now I really did need some tissues. So I walked through the nearest door and into my sister's bedroom. I wished my tears would turn into pins and lie buried in her carpet to pay her back.

Bedroom wasn't really the right word to describe my sister's private space. A friend of Dad's, who was a famous architect, had designed it to her precise specifications. She had gone for a sleek Japanese style. Everything was arranged so that it could be on hand to service her every need but could be hidden away. The large window had a long oak ledge with cupboards underneath. On the opposite wall there was a big mirror built in to a table and space for a hairdryer and make-up underneath. There were hidden screens that you could pull out to divide the space. One cupboard opened up into a study area with laptop, etc. Even the chocolate wrappers in the bin were folded neatly like origami and flattened down. There was no clutter anywhere. It was as if everything she did had a purpose and nothing was spontaneous. Her life was as impenetrable to me as the Hildegard motto: 'Appropriateness in partnership with academic achievement'.

I sat down on her bed and stroked the peach silk throw. I pulled one of the tissues from the box by the bedside table and blew my nose hard. As I was returning the box, I caught part of the silk throw in my sleeve and tugged it to the floor. As I reached out to grab it, I knocked the box of tissues under the bed. Then the delicate fabric seemed to wrap itself round my body and before I knew it I was falling off the bed with nothing but a handful of tissues for support.

The first time I tried to sit up I banged my head and slid down further on the floor. I managed to free a hand from underneath the fabric and grab the edge of the bed to haul myself up, as I freed my other hand and reached for the bed. This time there was no ridge to hold on to. There was an object in the way. It was a small black leather case.

My first thought was that it must be some kind of holder for contraceptives or something private like that.

One quick peek wouldn't do any harm.

It was a small knife with a patterned handle with a jewel in it. The most disturbing thing was that there were traces of a dark brown stuff on the end of the blade.

This knife had definitely been used.

As I was putting it back, I found a carefully folded up piece of paper with some sort of poem written on it.

Some people are fat on the inside
Secret layers of insulation
Coat their internal organs
Choking them slowly from the inside
Like a fat snake
Or a burger chain milkshake
But no one can see
No one can tell
That they aren't right
Or because they have a certain look
And money
No one cares
And they're left to despise
The outwardly fat or dumb
That's me
When I'm with Rosamund
I smile at her jokes, copy her look
Generally overrate her
She thinks I just go

Along with her
A pale imitator
If only I were brave enough
I'd like to
Cut
Her tongue out
One day I will
To show
How much
I *should*
Hate her

This was dynamite. Perfect revenge material. I sneaked it up to the den and made a copy with Dad's scanner.

Vix had acted out of spite, so why shouldn't I? So much for her being best mates with Rosamund. How two-faced is that? They had probably used the knife in some sort of sealing their friendship ritual. Either that or Vix was literally threatening to cut Rosamund's tongue out. So I would be doing Rosamund a favour in sending her the poem as well as getting my own back.

Without stopping to think I folded up the copy of the poem, popped it in an envelope, wrote Rosamund's name on it, and posted it through her front door on my way to the café.

Vix

We always have to be smarter than the rest
Academic success
Makes Mum feel better for being so rich
And furthers Dad's career
Now I really am being a bitch
I feel it today
That only the power of being mean
Can get you through
That being shallow
Stops you from
Drowning

Ava

Len was the first person to spot me. He was carrying a bowl full of dirty cups through to the kitchen. He clicked his heels and said, 'Reporting for duty.'

'Westwood sponge cake to be portioned, Ava.' Tasha put down a large sponge cake on the counter beside me. 'And make them size eight, not size sixteen, like you did last time.'

She handed me a knife. As I began slicing, my head buzzed with thoughts of my sister and how she had managed to spoil my work placement and what would happen next when Rosamund found the poem.

'Small slices I said, not bird table crumbs!'

'Sorry,' I muttered. 'I don't know what came over me.'

'I do.' Tasha shook her black bob decisively and went over to the kitchen and switched the radio off. 'Too much twang and drawl can rot the brain.'

Then six students came in from the nearby fashion college and spent ages deciding and then changing their minds on what coffee and cake to order. When we got them organised Tasha yelled, 'Coffee break time!'

I shook my head.

'Three times a laydeee!' Len crooned from the kitchen as he brought out the cups.

'All this stress is ageing me,' moaned Tasha. She reached into a small box on the table and took out her packet of stickies – apparently all the Hollywood stars of the past used the tape to tighten their skin and make lines disappear. When I tried them it made me feel as if my eyelashes were being lifted on top of my eyebrows.

'We need something to increase trade in the mornings. People don't fancy Versace cake and intense Coco Chanel bitter chocolate squares for breakfast every day.'

'How about a gluten free, non-animal fat, non-dairy breakfast muffin with lots of seeds and honey,' I suggested.

'Yes! I can see where you're going with this: The Stella McCartney Muffin! Pure genius.' Then she flashed her eyes at me and said, 'Spill, Ava.'

I looked around me and picked up a cloth. 'Where?'

She rolled her eyes. 'Very funny. Stop stalling and tell me why you were blubbing when you came in.'

'That was beads of sweat caused by extreme frustration.' I then explained about the work experience and how I'd overheard Mrs Berry talking about me.

Tasha clattered her coffee cup in its saucer. 'Those idiots wouldn't recognise true talent if it leaped up and bit them on the bum! We'll show them, Ava. We'll turn your placement here into something extraordinary.'

Len cheered from the kitchen, 'Yee ha, laydees!'

Tasha punched her arm up in triumph. 'I know! You can be the Cakewalk designer in residence. We'll put some of your dolls on display in the shop. We'll showcase them on the night of the prom party.'

'I have been working on something – I've been recreating some of Nan's favourite outfits and making shoebox-sized sets for them, but I'm not sure that anyone'd like them.'

'There's only one way to find out.' Tasha looked me in the face.

'We'll be too busy preparing the iced cakes order for the party,' I hedged.

'Quit stalling, Ava. I'm offering you a chance here. Are you going to take it?'

I nodded and we all shrieked 'YEE HA!'

Then Tasha began jumping up and introducing me to everyone in the café as her designer in residence. I felt my face go hot with embarrassment but I floated home on a little cloud of happiness. I couldn't wait to sit down and tell Dad my news. For once things had gone my way. I may have lost out on the Victoria and Albert Museum but I was going to have a chance to show my work. To show off Nan's dresses. I whooped like Nan had done when she'd finally shown someone Victor's photograph.

For once I'd outsmarted my sister. Bizarrely, that thought didn't fill me with joy, because of what I'd done to her. Acting on my feelings had made me feel shabby and ashamed of myself.

Vix

Small secret scar
Pressure valve
Touch the ridged place and it helps me to stay
    calm
And collected
Grace under pressure
I find myself looking at pieces of metal or pins
Any object that has the power to slice
Quickly
Rosamund asks me what I'm staring at
Nothing. I'm thinking about the future
Which is sort of true
'Pascal is dating a supermodel,' she tells me
As we drink our detox greens
'But he told me he really likes you.
You are honest and real.'
Inside I start to fill up
Emotions instead of food pile into my stomach
    and guts
'We need a special session,' Rosamund says

'It'll help us cope with the waiting
And we'll find a way to deal with you.'
I look up
Her eyes flicker
She smiles
'I mean
A way to deal with you and Pascal.'
I don't reply but I know that she is
Always right

Ava

We all got dressed up for a family dinner night. It was one of our unspoken rituals. Vix appeared in one of her many layered creations. I wanted to feel smart and efficient and slightly aloof so I wore a pencil skirt and button-up blouse with a large bow. Mum had changed from her crisp linen suit into a light summer dress with a pale blue cashmere cardigan. Dad was now wearing a bright checked shirt and was fiddling about trying to open a bottle of wine.

'Glass of wine?' Dad waved the bottle but Mum cut in.

'We've got orange juice or water if you'd prefer.'

'Not when you've gone to so much trouble selecting the perfect wine to go with the meal,' Vix said.

Dad bowed. 'Thank you for noticing. Nothing but the best for my beautiful and charming family.'

Vix raised her glass. 'I need some more wine after hearing that.'

'Both my daughters are growing up and it makes me feel ancient.' Dad grinned as he splashed a drop of wine in my glass.

Mum turned to Victoria. 'Soon you're off to Oxford, following in the family footsteps.'

Vix frowned. 'The results aren't out yet. My grades might not be up to scratch.'

'Nonsense. You're the brains of this family and we expect great things from our brilliant daughter.' Mum beamed. 'Nothing less than perfection for Victoria!'

I turned to Dad. 'I thought university was about falling in love with lots of people. Wasn't it like that when you and Mum were at college?'

'Please don't say anything incriminating, Alan.' My mum tried to sound light-hearted.

'It was an interesting time to be a student and of course there was no such thing as a student loan in those days. Everything was free,' Dad replied.

'And most of us didn't realise how lucky we were.' Mum sighed. 'Katy was always good at reminding us of that, wasn't she? I remember how shocked we so-called liberals were when she announced that she was going into a convent.'

'But then we had our finals and we fell in love and the girls came along.' Dad's face glowed with all the recollections.

'Enough!' Mum squirmed. Was she afraid that he was going to spill the secret of the real date of their wedding?

'All this talk of the past has made me hungry. Let's eat,'

Dad said diplomatically, taking the lid off the Thai curry dish.

There was a pause and everyone began grabbing at bowls of food and commenting on each dish.

'Irene is a great cook,' Dad said.

'She is always grumbling about how much everything costs.' Vix laughed.

'That's because things don't just fall into her lap like for some people. Her daughter is at university in America. We are helping out with the fees – something that you don't have to worry about, Victoria,' Mum said a little defensively.

'Let's not forget Ava's artistic talent.' Dad looked over at me. 'She is going to have an exhibition of her work at the café where she'll be doing her work experience,' Dad said.

'I thought you said you were going to the Victoria and Albert Museum?' Mum asked.

'Kennedy was considered more suitable for that one.' I looked my sister full in the face.

Vix looked surprised.

'Are you OK, Vix?' I said, and added under my breath, 'Looks like someone's poked you with a knife.'

Vix's face froze.

'What are you talking about?' asked Mum joining in the conversation. 'What's this about a knife?'

'There's no knife. I was speaking metaphorically and

got it wrong. I think I meant to say something about someone looking daggers at me.'

Everybody laughed apart from Vix and the conversation turned to world politics. After dinner everybody else went into the sitting room, but I mumbled something about having to do coursework and went to my room.

I snuggled up on the bed with the packets of Nan's dress patterns. It was the next best thing to have her holding me in her arms. And I really needed her. Seeing that expression on Vix's face when I'd mentioned the word knife had shaken me up. Who was she trying to hurt with that knife and why? Did she really hate Rosamund that much that she would try to cut her? No wonder Lady Macbeth went mad under the strain of keeping her guilty secrets.

I was still trying to figure it out when I got the text from Vix.

She was going to come to my room in five minutes for a meeting. It was five past midnight.

Vix

Ava
I want to say something kind to my sister
Ease her pain a bit
Tell her I understand about Nan
But my tongue has a sharp tip
The ugliness is filling up inside of me again
Overflowing cesspit
And I'm incapable of it
When I think about the future
I'm afraid
The present is unreal
If you want something badly enough it has to
        happen
Doesn't it?
And when the feelings of wanting mix with fear
        and disgust
Build up a plaque on the soul
I have to do
Something
To release the fear

Maybe I should
Explain about the knife
And how it's nothing to be afraid of
That it's saving
My life

Ava

When I'm in my room with its overflowing plastic bags of fabric scraps, my pincushion collection, my shelf of Barbies and my collage wall of 1970s knitting patterns, I feel like I'm in control of my life.

No one comes in here, not even Irene who has refused to clean it saying, 'I don't know what rubbish you want to keep and what to throw away!'

Before Rosamund and Kennedy had come back on the scene Vix would often come in to sit and talk. Nothing too deep, just comforting chat, or we'd sit and paint our toenails together.

That night Vix had taken off all her make-up and her hair was scrunched back into a tight ponytail. She was wearing just a large, oversized grey sweater top that would make most people look like a sack of potatoes but looked stylish on her. She walked over to the window seat and sat herself down hugging her knees up to her chest. Her toenails were perfectly manicured and painted a deep vermilion.

'You've smeared a bit.' I pointed to the top of her leg where I noticed a red splodge.

Vix flushed and said quickly, 'I cut myself trying to shave my legs with that new razor. Agony. I'll never use it again. I came to say that I'm sorry if I inadvertently messed up your work experience by talking about it to Kennedy and I wanted to ask you if you'd reconsider helping me. Will you help me make my evening dress for the prom party? I'd like something vintage and with long sleeves. I can't find anything I like. Most evening gowns are usually sleeveless. I hate my arms. They are too fleshy.'

'Purleese.' I groaned. 'What is Rosamund wearing?'

'She is going for a Pre-Raphaelite medieval princess cut with a modern twist.'

'She could end up looking like a nun!' I snorted.

'Not with the low cleavage on her design,' Vix said, laughing.

'I suppose the flesh has to be exposed somewhere.'

'You're the expert at flesh.' She looked at me.

I instinctively covered my tummy with my hand. There was a pause. I sniffed and my voice became cold and business-like. 'I usually work from a pattern. Then I'll need to take your measurements and choose a fabric. I'll have to work quickly because there's not much time to make it but Miss Duncan thinks it will be good for my portfolio.'

'There is just over a month to the prom party. Can you do it in time?'

'It would be a lot of work, but I could just about do it. That's if you choose a simple pattern for me to follow.

A little black dress or something like that.'

She came over to the bed and picked up one of Nan's precious dress patterns.

'What are these?'

'Some patterns that I haven't sorted yet.' I didn't want her to touch them, but she'd already untied the ribbon and laid out the packets randomly on the bed.

'That one,' she said decisively. 'But not in a light colour – a deep red would be good.' She waggled her toes.

My heart sank. It was the one pattern that I could hardly bring myself to look at let alone make up.

'That's a wedding dress pattern.'

'It's beautiful.' Vix picked up the packet and looked at the picture. 'So perfect for the prom party. No one else will have a dress like this.'

'I'm not sure I can make it in time,' I mumbled.

'Please don't let me down, Ava. I know things haven't been great between us lately but it would mean a lot if you could help me.' She bent down to give me a hug and added, 'I'll get the fabric tomorrow.'

Just as she was leaving I asked, 'Is everything all right?'

She paused. 'Why shouldn't it be?' she said in a quiet voice.

'No reason,' I lied.

I had to find out what had happened to the note I'd sent to Rosamund. Things had gone too quiet and the air felt charged, like the calm before a storm.

Ava

The next morning Kennedy looked surprised to see me when she answered the door.

'Do you want to see my sister? I was just going to take Precious out for a walk.' Her eyes narrowed suspiciously.

'I've come to see you,' I said.

She smiled. 'Great! It was just that I thought you'd come to see Rosamund. I recognised your handwriting on that note your pushed through our letterbox.'

She kept me waiting for ages whilst she fussed with the lead and made sure she got the right colour doggy hair clip for Precious to match her jacket.

'Are you sure you want to come with us? It's pretty boring. I mean, I just throw a ball, we sit on a bench that sort of thing,' she said as we headed to the park.

'I need to talk to you about something.'

'If it's about the work experience . . .'

'No, I don't want to talk about that. It was pretty low, mean and spiteful of you to nab my placement but I'm over it now. Tasha is making me her designer in residence and letting me use the café to exhibit some of my stuff.'

'That's brilliant. I'll help you if you like.'

I glared at her. Did that girl have no shame? She did look genuinely pleased for me though.

'I suppose I'll be too busy. I'm sorry about the placement. Mum can be pretty ruthless when it comes to her daughters. I thought that we'd both be able to work there.'

'So it was your mum that got it all changed?' I gasped. This was news to me.

'Yes, when Vix told us about the V&A being an option, my mum thought it would be good for me too. I didn't realise there was only one place.'

'So Vix did tell you about my placement then?' I was starting to feel more confused.

'Yes, she did, and I was really hurt. I thought we were friends. I told you about my plans and you were always so vague about yours.'

'I'm sorry. It was just that it was too important to me to speak about. If I said it out loud I thought I might ruin it.'

We sat down on a bench in the square and watched the dog for a while. 'How's Vix's prom dress going?' Kennedy asked. 'Mum is tearing her hair out as Rosamund keeps changing her mind on the design, plus she's never around to try the thing on and the dressmaker charges by the hour.'

'I'm helping Vix with hers,' I said.

'It'll be brilliant then. Soon they'll both be away at university. I'm looking forward to having a bit of space to myself,' Kennedy continued. 'These last few years have been tough. As soon as I got used to a school we would have to move on.'

'Why was that?'

Kennedy shifted in her seat. 'Mum says it's because Rosamund sets herself such high standards and some girls get jealous. They made up stuff about her and some parents blamed her when other girls stopped eating, too. They said she exerted an influence, but that's just crazy, isn't it? Rosamund can't help it if people want to be like her. She is the type of person that people seem to gravitate towards. I thought you wanted to be her friend when you sent her that letter.'

I picked up a stick and hurled it in the air and we both watched Precious race after it, twisting himself into somersaults trying to catch it.

'Look what she's done for Vix. Got her into the Gifted and Talented Group. Helped her with her personal style as well as with her choice of university. Fixed her up with Pascal too, but you know all about that.' She gave me a knowing look.

'I don't.'

Kennedy frowned. 'But you sent her that note. Rosamund said that you wrote to her and asked her to fix Vix up with Pascal. Pascal is a family friend and he often comes round. Rosamund told him that Vix was crazy about him and that you had told her so. Isn't that what you wrote?'

Now I was stuck. I couldn't tell Kennedy what was really in that envelope. But why would Rosamund lie like that? Maybe she was such a good friend of Vix's that she didn't believe what she read in the note and made up the Pascal story to let me off the hook. What if I'd misjudged her?

'I sent her some of Vix's personal stuff and I don't think it was about Pascal,' I said slowly. 'Kennedy, sending that letter was a big mistake. I can't say too much but can you let Rosamund know that it was a mistake?'

Kennedy sighed and said, 'I'll try. So your sister doesn't like Pascal, then?'

'No. Yes. I'm not sure.'

'Pascal is gorgeous but he can be a bit sleazy. He thinks of women as a recreational activity. He says that if someone throws themselves at him they deserve all they get.'

'Do you think Rosamund will put him straight about Vix?'

Kennedy frowned. 'Rosamund is complicated. Something in that letter you sent made her cross with Vix. If she thinks someone has slighted her in any way she has to pay them back. She doesn't lose her temper. Rosamund says that, "Revenge is a dish best served cold." Are you all right?'

I nodded. 'Just feel a bit chilled.'

'At one of the boarding schools we went to she found out that this girl, Esme, had been saying mean things about her, so Rosamund went out of her way to be her friend. Then she got hold of this photo of Esme when she was fatter and stuffing herself with cake and Rosamund used the photo for her art project and copied it on to a large canvas.'

'Wow! That was mean!'

'Rosamund told me she hadn't realised it would affect her that much.'

'Did you believe her when she said that?'

'I don't always believe everything she says. I have a mind of my own. For instance, she thinks you are a bit unhinged whereas I think of you as a friend. We both do.' She picked up Precious, who had come back, and lifted his paw and said in a baby voice, 'Will you be friends with us, Ava?'

I nodded. I was going to need all the friends I could get when all this mess unravelled.

Ava

There is something about sewing at night that comforts me. The closed curtains and the glow of the lamp, the faint sound of cotton pulling through satin makes me feel calm and full of hope, like a romantic heroine. After that conversation with Kennedy I needed to be alone. All the threads of my life were tangled and I didn't know which one to pull to smooth everything out, so I decided to start with Nan.

Every time I read Victor's letter it made me think about love. People tell you how it's supposed to be a squashy-pink-fluffy-cloud sort of emotion but from what I've seen it's pretty raw. Romeo and Juliet have to die, Cathy and Heathcliff's passion turns to destructive hatred. My sister had a crush on Pascal. I think I'll give love a wide berth.

I had found a large piece of 60s floral print in an Oxfam shop and used it to make up a Barbie miniature of the summer dress. There was so much fabric I was going to make myself a dress out of it. That was going to be my next full-size dressmaking project. It would have to wait until all the miniatures of Nan's dresses had been made.

I finished sewing the hem of the prom dress and floated it carefully over my tailor's dummy. Vix's dress was coming along nicely, even if it was hard to literally pin her down. Tonight she was at Salvador's yet again. Since she had finished her exams, she went out nearly every evening. I was making great progress with constructing and was planning on finishing it tonight. I just needed a bit of matching thread. There was some in Nan's shoebox, but it was caught in the box lining.

The bottom of the shoebox was lined with ancient Christmas paper that had some sort of padding underneath. The sellotape that was holding it had long come unstuck. I carefully took the padding out. It contained a bit of an old Weetabix packet cut out with a shopping list scribbled on the back in Nan's rounded handwriting. Underneath that was an envelope that was addressed to Nan at the canteen. I recognised Victor's handwriting. So there had been another letter!

I do not have much time so please forgive the rushed nature of this letter, only I was very keen to seize this opportunity to get word to you. You are often in my thoughts and all the happy times we spent together last year are a great comfort to me during this difficult time. People ask me why I am smiling like a fool but I do not tell them it is

*because I am picturing you in your bright summer
dress handing me a bowl of rice pudding.*

*The Government is in chaos at the moment and
there is a real chance that a civil war will break out.
There is also a chance that it won't and that soon I'll
be able to resume my studies in Manchester. I cannot
believe that it is over a year since we last saw each
other. How is the job? I hope that no other student
has captured your attention. I have a cousin who has
married an Englishman and moved to Birmingham.
Her name is Esther and her address is 21a Erith
Terrace. You can contact me through her. I await
your response in eager anticipation.*

Forever Yours, with much love,
Victor

So Victor had tried to keep in touch with Nan but she had
already promised her family that she wouldn't contact
him or else she would be forced to give up Mum. What a
mess! All this stuff was coming out too late. I'd promised
Nan that I wouldn't talk to Mum about it. Mum wasn't
interested in her 'so-called' father anyway.

But I had to do something.

I could write a letter and send it to that address.
Victor should know how Nan felt about him and why she
hadn't been able to contact him. If he was still alive, of
course. I could do that for Nan. There was always a slim

chance that Victor's cousin lived at the same address. I had to give it a try.

As I posted the letter I felt like a shipwrecked sailor sending out a message in a bottle clinging on to the hope of rescue.

Ava

Mum was arranging oranges in the crystal bowl. She placed each fruit with care as if she were creating a still life painting. The late afternoon sun backlit her hair and made her part of the composition. I couldn't help wondering how she'd felt about marrying Dad, knowing that he had loved somebody else. Angry, sad, betrayed or relieved? And if it made her think about Nan and how she had been left pregnant with her.

She turned to me and said, 'You're late, Ava. Your Mind Games class ended at five p.m.'

I sighed. 'I stopped at the café to have a coffee with Tasha.'

'Decaffeinated, I hope.'

'The oranges look nice,' I said.

She sniffed and removed one from the group. 'That's better. More balanced.' She stood back, took one more look at the oranges, and sat down at the kitchen table. 'How are you getting on with Vix's dress?'

'I was having some problems getting the seams under the arms right but Tasha gave me some ideas,' I said, sitting down opposite her.

'Are you sure you're up to this? Vix needs to look her best. We can always bring in a professional seamstress to finish it.'

She pushed one of my curls from out of my face.

I bit down on the side of my cheek and said slowly, 'I think I'm up to it.'

'Prom party is a showcase. *Tatler* covers it and there will be a lot of interest.' Mum tapped her fingers on the table. 'And I won't be there because I have to go to Geneva first thing in the morning instead of next week. Do you think Vix will mind?'

Since Nan had died she had taken on heaps of extra work. Her face was etched with stress lines and her eyes were puffy with grief so I replied, 'She won't mind.'

Mum's features relaxed a bit. 'Your father will be here and I'll help settle her in at Oxford.'

She picked up the bowl and carried it carefully into the sitting room where I was sure that it would be placed on the sideboard with real care and precision.

I waited until I could hear Mum going upstairs and then I crept into the sitting room and 'unbalanced' the oranges in the crystal bowl. Too much precision makes me nauseous. That's why I prefer Gothic architecture with its twisty turrets to sleak modernism.

After the orange tampering, I went up to the mosh pit that is my room. It was a relief to close the door on order

147

and hurl myself on my bed. I lay on my back and scanned the room. I was feeling 'itchy' like I didn't really fit into my skin. I suppose it takes years before you feel really comfortable with yourself.

No one ever questioned the fact that Vix was going to get top marks in all her exams, but everything I did was always followed by comments like, 'Did you do that by yourself, Ava? Miss Duncan helped you, didn't she?' or 'Ava is my non-academic daughter.'

Why don't they just stick pins in me and have done with it!

In my Mind Games class, our instructor would say, 'Be in the moment. Don't think about anything else. Focus!'

As soon as I heard those instructions I'd start to get hot and panicky as if the moment were an icy precipice that I was about to slide off and the only safe place to be was back in time in another place in your head.

A place where you can't slip up.

Ava

'You are so clever. Vix will look beautiful in this.' Dad had come into my room to inspect the infamous prom dress.

'That's not saying much. She'd look good in anything.' I sniffed. My sister didn't need to carry a knife to hurt me. Dad never passed any comment on anything that I wore.

'I'm planning a surprise. I'm going to show up at the hotel in Geneva and whizz Elspeth off for a holiday. She's been under a lot of pressure lately. What do you think?'

Suddenly everybody wants to know my opinion, I thought, but out loud I said, 'What about the prom party?'

'I'm sure that Vix will have a better time without her parents breathing down her neck.'

I chewed on my lip and wondered if now was a good time to share with him some of my secrets. He would be less angry than Mum at what I'd done and probably more understanding. He worked in Government and they were used to leaks and documents turning up where they weren't supposed to be. He would probably know lots of ways to cover things up.

I took a deep breath and half closed my eyes in preparation to speak when Dad broke the moment and said, 'We'd better get down to the kitchen or we'll be late for supper and I'm starving.'

Jonathon came rushing in to the kitchen after us carrying a pile of clothes, followed by Mum with a washing basket full of clothes.

'Last minute call for the charity shop collection!'

'I like that shirt!' Dad picked out a faded check one from the basket

'Alan, it's all frayed at the cuffs.'

'I like to potter around the house in it.' Dad clung to the shirt like a baby to a security blanket.

Mum pondered and then said, 'All right.'

Jonathon put the clothes down on the kitchen table and began folding the rest of the contents as Vix came in. He held up a T-shirt and said, 'Vix, there are seven short sleeved T-shirts of yours in the charity shop pile, is that right?'

'You've never worn some of them. They've still got their price tags attached,' said Mum, picking one up in her hand.

'Then the poor people who get them will be really happy.'

Mum frowned. 'Decadence and selfishness never made anyone happy.'

Without thinking I said, 'If pride must abide.' There was a pause. It had been one of Nan's sayings.

'Mum, I can't worry about charity shop piles at the moment, I've got too much on organising the party. Tonight we're meeting with Pascal to discuss the layout of the back bar.'

Vix

Rosamund is late
I text her
No reply
Pascal can't wait
He needs to do a sound check
And order stock
He drinks coffee
And smiles at me
I need to think of layouts
Not way outs
Because tomorrow
One way or the other
When I open that piece of paper
My life changes
Just as we're finishing
Finalising
DJs and Champagne
Rosamund arrives
And makes us do it all again
I glance over at Pascal

I check again
Look closely into his eyes
He suggests a drive
To clear our minds
Rosamund bails
'Important stuff to do.'
I implore with a big-eyed look
That she chooses to ignore
I sigh
Wait for the knock back
He grins
'It'll be a laugh.'
So it's Pascal and me
And London
On a summer night
Sparkles
We drive along the Embankment
Flick open the sunroof
'I can't wait to be living my own life.'
I want to get a reaction
But nothing comes
Pascal drives faster
Later on
In Pascal's car
On the edge of
Hampstead Heath
Pascal calls my bluff

About
Living my life
Perfect for a second
I can feel it
Nothing matters for a second
Then he
Pulls away
'It's me, not you,' he says
But I see the look
Disgust
And I don't blame
Him
Then I want
To shame
Him
To hurt him with words
To make him feel
As small as I am
So I tell him
I have another man
And he is ice cold
Rosamund would approve
I suppose you can call
What we had just done
Consensual
Sex
After all

Rosamund gave me the go ahead
If my heart didn't
Going on and on
About him
Like he was a prize
A top mark to aspire to
An object
To channel your desire through
So what if my heart wasn't in it?
Afterwards
I invest more meaning
Into what we've done
Picture a romance complete with dates
But all Pascal wants
Is my picture?
At least I'm not alone
The 'gallery' on Pascal's
Mobile phone
My stupid face
Has bags of company
I don't care
Pretend
That I don't care
About losing control
And
Giving someone vile
The chance to share me

Like a cheap joke
For people I don't know to look at me
And know something I did
That I'm not proud of
That my life is now like
A comment on an essay
'Could do better.'
Time to find the
One who is cold and hard
And jealously discreet
Who takes me away from myself
Every time we meet

Ava

I heard the sound of Mum's cab outside the house at around five a.m. An hour later another taxi appeared to take Dad. I decided to give Vix's dress a final iron. I turned it inside out and carefully pressed the seams down.

Deep down I knew that part of me had resented Vix for picking out the pattern. By doing that she had somehow snooped on me and Nan. Irrational because she didn't know about Nan, and Victor. It was me who knew how much Victor loved her. I was the one who knew about Nan and I was the one who could make her wedding dress for her.

I picked up Victor's letters. Every time I read them I felt better. One day Mum might feel the same. If only Nan's parents had seen the second letter they might have changed their minds.

Vix would look perfect in the dress. All she had to do was collect her results and shine at the prom party. She would put Pascal and Rosamund in their places.

The iron was cool enough now to press the miniature dresses. I still hadn't made up my mind about the final box – was I going to dress the doll in the piece of cotton with Victor's words written on them or would a naked doll be in the box? I couldn't make my mind up.

At around seven-thirty I heard sounds of Vix's power shower turning off, so I went down to the kitchen and cut myself a huge slab of bread to have with chocolate spread and was musing about how to arrange the setting for the fifth and final cabinet.

Vix came down and poured herself a glass of water.

'You're early,' I said.

'What do you mean?' she snapped at me as she opened her handbag and fumbled for something. Her hands were shaking as she churned over the contents of her bag: large wallet, keys, small black case, before she found her cigarettes.

'Mum will kill you if you smoke in the house.'

'She's not here.'

'You'll set off the smoke alarm.'

Vix put the packet away and sipped at her drink.

'Smoking gives you wrinkles,' I said.

'Not today, Ava. I can't cope with your inane prattle today.'

'I need to see what your dress looks like on. I'm working late at the café. There won't be time to do any last minute alterations.'

'Just leave it on my bed,' Vix said as she was leaving the room. 'Thanks.'

Vix

Today I order
A thick hot chocolate
With cream
Not to drink
To hold in my hands
And inhale its promise
My phone is alive
With text messages
The bright-eyed
Ones who are
Sure
Because they have kept their minds
On simple things
Not the bigger picture
But like a thread pulled
From a seam
Like a Victorian heroine
I am undone
The melodrama makes
Me smile

'You'll be all right,
You always get what you want
You'll be good enough.'
The chocolate smell tries to
Comfort
I'll be fine
I pinch my arm
If I want my results badly enough
It has to happen
Doesn't it?
Time to go to school and find out
Then
Drive back home
To dress
For success
Even if your life is a mess
Ava is a genius
The dress is beautiful
The satin feels soft against my skin
The colour is perfect
I put it on and swirl around the room
Too perfect to wear to the party
Where people would stare and say
Never mind
This is not a never mind dress

Ava

Len was outside the café washing Tasha's ancient camper van, and inside every available space was filled with iced cupcakes. The sweet smell was comforting. We had spent the whole day preparing food for the party. At around six o'clock there was one last job to be done.

Tasha handed me an icing gun and a list as she said in cowboy-speak, 'OK, pardner, get shooting.'

Each cake had to have a girl's name iced on it and then sprinkled with sugar stars. Then all the cake tins and bowls of solidified icing sugar had to be washed up.

'I hope those spoiled madams appreciate this,' Tasha said as she furiously scrubbed a bowl.

'They are probably all on diets and won't touch them,' Len said, coming into the kitchen, sniffing.

'If I didn't need the business so much I'd turn up and hurl the cakes at them,' Tasha said.

I gave a mock cough. 'May I remind you that you have one of Hildegard's finest amongst you? Please feel free to hurl cakes in my direction.'

'Ava, darling, you are an artist and therefore set apart from that weird bunch.'

'I'll take that as a compliment.'

Tasha flicked me with a tea towel. 'Believe me it is. At one of the many private schools that I went to, all the so-called pretty and smart girls were getting the school involved in a sick non-eating competition, but I was the one labelled the troublemaker for dyeing my hair pink. I lost count of the number of times people wished I could be more like them. When all the time they were starving themselves to death and awarding themselves points for it! At that school you even had to be the best at destroying yourself! I tried to tell people, but who would listen to the "jealous troublemaker".'

'Do you think that sort of stuff still goes on?' I said, thinking about Vix and Rosamund.

'Probably,' Tasha said as we were rearranging the tables and chairs.

The café door opened and Kennedy came in. 'You couldn't spare me a cup of coffee only I've been at work experience all day.'

'I'll get it,' I responded.

'Skinny latte decaff,' she said.

'Full fat Americano or nothing,' I replied, putting a mug down beside her.

'It's like a madhouse at home. Screaming and phoning, tears and hysteria.'

'Did Rosamund do badly in her exams?' I asked, trying not to show how pleased that would make me feel.

Kennedy smiled. 'Mum is opening Champagne but I'm feeling too exhausted to celebrate.'

Tasha winked at me and said, 'That's terrible. Are they working you too hard?'

Kennedy sighed. 'It's so boring. Most of the time I have to input data on a computer and you have to handle the clothes so carefully and be nagged all the time. I wish I'd got your placement here. At least you have a laugh.'

I suppose I should've been angry with her but what would have been the point?

'Oh my God. I am so insensitive,' Kennedy said, putting her hand over her mouth.

'I don't mind about the work experience . . .' I started to say but Kennedy cut in.

'What's it been like at your place today?' she asked in a very dramatic voice.

'Pretty quiet, I guess,' I replied.

Kennedy looked at me and nodded. 'I suppose things would be a bit subdued.'

Len put on his battered old combat jacket. 'Let's go and pick up your stuff,' he said.

As Kennedy was leaving she turned to me and said in a pitying voice, 'Send Vix my love. It's not the end of the world! Not everyone can be like Rosamund.'

Everything went *kerching* in my head as all the rows matched up in the fruit machine that is my brain.

Except it was a row of knives and not lemons.

Vix

Arrive home
Switch off phone
Empty gesture
As no one has called
Or will do
Take long shower
And put on dress again
Its perfection mocks
Me
Perfect colour
In the sitting room
My bare toes
Perfectly manicured
Wiggle on the thick carpet
Stare into space
Until sunlight
Falls into place
On crystal glass
And oranges
My finger traces the edges

And taps out its ring tone
Pure and clear
Clear and pure
Its chime
Vibrates around the room
I raise it up with both hands
Feel like goddess in flowing dress
Raised so high
And then smash
And rip the seam on the sleeves
So it flaps
Take up a diamond
And lose myself
In adrenaline rush
Until I see your face
Looking at me

Ava

As I walked into the room the noise hit me. A sound that was part laughter and part scream. It filled the air like a bad smell. So I clamped my hands to my ears as my eyes darted around the room.

I saw my sister Vix, who was lying on the sofa with her eyes fixed on the middle distance. Her lips were pursed into an ironic grin and on her arm there was a crisscross of cuts like matching self-satisfied smiles. One of the larger cuts was a gushing smile. I watched its slow and steady progress on the cream linen sofa. Looking back I know it was madness, but at the time I was sure that Vix winked at me, so I winked back.

At her feet lay the pieces of the Georgian crystal fruit bowl and several oranges.

The sun shifted from behind a cloud and unexpectedly lit up the room. My body felt heavy but my head was a helium balloon cut off from the action and floating above everything. Only that incessant noise kept dragging me back to that room. It was a torture of noise followed by a relief of silence and then relentlessly back again to the noise.

Vix smacked her lips. It was as if all the energy in the room had sucked all the moisture out of her. Her feet nudged some of the oranges that had fallen from the bowl.

'Eat an orange,' I wanted to say. 'It'll help.' But that screeching noise got in the way of words. That wailing noise was drilling into my brain. Would it never stop? I tried to blot it out. I shifted my feet and touched some of the pieces of the lead crystal that had once been the fruit bowl.

All this must have happened in a matter of seconds, but it felt like hours as my brain struggled to process the scene before my eyes and gear itself up for some actions.

Before I could do anything, the door opened and Len charged into the room.

The wailing noise continued.

Len went over to the sideboard and lifted up the bunch of lilies from the large glass vase. He held the flowers in their carefully arranged shape and I thought he was going to bow and present them to Vix, but he threw them on the floor scattering their staining pollen all over the carpet.

Len and the vase spun around towards me and a split second later the tepid water hit me full in the face. I blinked as the glutinous stinking water stung my eyes. As Len put the vase back he said, 'Shut the f*** up, Ava!'

I was about to complain about his swearing – he wasn't allowed to in the café – when I registered that the wailing had stopped.

It had been coming from me!

I'd been soaking up other people's secrets until they had burst out of me like a high-pitched glass-splintering note.

Ava

I stared at myself in the hall mirror for a long time. The slimy water was running in small rivulets down my back. My eyes burned back at me like an accusing stranger. I lifted my hands to my face. Like a child playing 'Peepo', I was hoping that maybe, just maybe, if I covered my face in my hands and closed my eyes then I could make all the bad things disappear. But when I looked again things were exactly the same.

I was feeling queasy and my throat hurt like hell. I was numb and manic at the same time.

I walked out to the camper van. Vix was sitting hunched inside and Len was standing on the gravel path.

'Len, shall I call for an ambulance?'

I watched as his swollen fingers performed the delicate task of sprinkling tobacco on the fine paper and rolling himself a cigarette.

'We'll take her to the Commanding Officer. Damage limitation.'

After he had licked the paper he looked up and offered it to me.

'It can help when you've been in a combat situation or had a shock.' He smiled at me.

I shook my head.

Len stepped away from me. 'Ava, you stink!'

I pulled away some green sludge from my hair. 'Fermenting flower water.'

He nodded. 'I should've slapped you. Had to knock a soldier clean out once because he'd lost it and would've given us away to the Argies. Haven't lost my touch, have I?'

His tone of voice changed and he addressed a shrub. 'What have we here then? You're a disgrace, soldier. Billy, the regimental goat, looks smarter than you!'

Len always seemed to be balancing himself between extreme moments of clarity or craziness. It must be his way of keeping himself from feeling too much pain. I expected him to be a fast and reckless driver but he drove carefully.

Vix groaned. 'I feel sick.'

I finally persuaded Len to pull over so she could throw up in the gutter.

We took her round the back entrance of the café and bundled her up the stairs.

'Don't touch me!' Vix yelled as Tasha dabbed her with iodine a few minutes later.

The muscle at the side of Tasha's cheek twitched as she kept on dabbing the stinging ointment on to my big sister's pale body but she didn't say a word. My throat still burned from the screaming.

Tasha put her in the spare bedroom with a hot water bottle and she fell fast asleep.

'Drink this, Ava,' Len poked a large mug in front of me. 'It's got sugar, lemon, whisky and hot water in it. It'll make you feel better.'

'I am so dumb. I could have worked this out sooner. I knew that my sister was up to something. I knew that things weren't right.' I raked my fingers through my hair and tugged at the ends.

Tasha's eyes flashed at me. 'Don't blame yourself. We're all up to something we shouldn't be.' She banged her fist on the table. I had never seen her so angry before.

She got up. 'Len and I have to deliver the cakes. I also promised Pascal I'd help serve so I won't be back until late. Keep an eye on your sister. Don't worry, I won't say anything, but we will have to think about contacting your parents later.'

'I'm sorry, Tasha.'

'I'm not mad at you, Ava. I'm not even mad at your sister. I'm just mad about the situation, that's all! We'll talk in the morning.'

I sat in silence at the table sipping my drink and trying not to think for as long as I could.

Then I curled up on the sofa and fell asleep.

Vix

I have a lover
Unlike any other
Cold and hard and cruel
But he makes me feel better
Than I am
He takes me to a place
Where pain doesn't matter
He keeps me in control
See a pin
Stick it in
And I will always follow him
He won't kill me at least
Not just yet
I wake up
And I try to reopen one of my marks
Because it will stop me
From moving on with my thoughts
Shame is a cruel-hearted woman
Who pecks at my cheek
Like an old auntie

Peck peck peck
Until I am down to size
Small and trembling
Ridiculous and weak
Not smart
No heart
Only plenty of blood
Tasha pops her head round the door
And smiles, 'Cup of tea?'
I slip on my mask
Smile back
Yes please

Ava

It was weird to think that the prom party was taking place across the road. It seemed like Vix and I were trapped in a bubble in Tasha's flat where everything was unreal until we stepped out into the street and set our lives in motion again.

This was all wrong. Vix was supposed to get fantastic A-level grades and I was supposed to have put up my exhibition in the café. I felt a pang thinking about all my artwork still bundled in the back of the camper van, but there was nothing I could do about it.

The next thing I remembered was Tasha pulling the curtains open and leaving me with a mug of tea.

Downstairs I could hear the sound of Len's country and western radio station blasting out. It seemed so normal until the memory of Vix on the sofa made me sit bolt upright.

I got up and went into the spare bedroom. Vix was sitting on the edge of the bed, picking at her arms and crying.

'Does it hurt?' I came and sat down beside her.

'A bit,' she said. I noticed that she was still wearing the

prom dress even though the sleeves were torn and splattered with blood.

'Did you want to die?' I asked.

She shook her head. 'Only inside. I wanted to kill the pain. Getting my lousy A-level grades was the final straw. You won't understand.' She roughly wiped some snot from the edge of her nose. I passed her a tissue from the box by the bed and she blew her nose loudly. 'I'm a mess and I've ruined the dress and it was so beautiful.'

'I suppose some dresses are just destined never to be made,' I said, and explained that the pattern she had chosen was going to be Nan's wedding dress.

Vix began to cry again. 'That's so sad.'

I noticed that she was shivering. I went into the sitting room and borrowed one of Tasha's shawls. Vix's body trembled as I put it across her shoulders.

'I hope I don't bleed on it.'

'You should be OK if you don't unpick any more of the bandages.'

'I feel so stupid. I just got carried away. I was angry. Do you think Mum and Dad know?'

'Tasha said she would call them this morning but she hasn't said anything and I haven't contacted them yet.'

'They will be ringing this morning for the exam results. They said they'd wait until after the prom party. I can't face them. Not yet.'

She looked panic-stricken, so to distract her I told her

about my last meeting with Nan and what she'd told me about Victor.

'And you haven't told Mum? She's going to be wiped out by this news. It'll be cool to know something about our grandfather.'

'He might even still be alive,' I said. 'Then we could all go out and visit him in Africa – when we know what country.'

'Nan didn't tell you which country he was from by any chance?'

I shook my head.

The doorbell downstairs rang. Vix froze. I looked out of the window. 'It's only Pascal. He's returning some baking trays by the looks of things. He looks rough. Must have been a good night.'

'Is he coming in? I do not want to see him.' A note of panic rose in her voice.

'Rosamund didn't try to set you up with him, did she?' I said, remembering what Kennedy had said.

Vix did not need to say anything. The look on her face said it had happened.

It was my turn to crumple and reach for the tissue box.

'I was so mad at you when I thought that you'd stopped my work experience that I did something terrible.'

'What did you do, Ava?'

'I can't say. I'm too ashamed. Ouch!'

Vix had picked up the box of tissues and bashed me

on the side of the head with it.

'TELL ME WHAT YOU DID, AVA!'

'I sent Rosamund one of your poems. The one about how much you hated her. I felt so bad afterwards.'

Vix slapped me on the cheek.

'When was that? When?'

'Hey, there's no need to hit me. It was when I found out about the work experience.'

I saw the look in Vix's eyes and picked up the box of tissues in self-defence and waved them in the air as threateningly as I could.

'So Rosamund set me up with Pascal to pay me back.'

'Not much of a friend.'

'Not much of a sister. You slimy snoop, you haven't got a life of your own so you spy on other people's!'

I bopped her on the head with the tissue box.

'I do not. Take that back!'

She wrenched the box out of my hands and started bashing me whilst I fended her off with slaps.

We ended up in a boxer's bear hug, each clinging on to the other. I thought about biting her to make her stop when I realised that her whole body was convulsing with sobs.

I relaxed my grip. Vix rested her head on my shoulders. When I looked round she was laughing silently and hysterically.

Some feelings are so extreme that you either have to laugh or explode.

Jonathon and Tasha were standing in the doorway and they joined in with the laughter. 'What a sight for sore eyes,' Tasha said.

'Such devoted sisters.' Jonathon arched an eyebrow and then, when he saw Vix's arms, his expression changed and he came over and carefully hugged her.

'I couldn't decide what to do, so I rang Jonathon and asked for his advice,' said Tasha.

'I've rung your parents and said that you had a bit of an accident with the crystal bowl but that you're OK. They'll be back this afternoon.'

'Thanks, Jonathon,' I said.

'I've made us all a huge breakfast downstairs,' Tasha said.

As we all went down to the kitchen, I realised that I was starving hungry.

'Rosamund is an evil witch,' I said as I stabbed at my bacon.

'Did she get her into this?' Tasha asked me. 'I knew it. Those high achieving girls' schools are the pits. Breeding grounds for weird obsessions.'

'Will you stop talking about me as if I was an imbecile?' Vix said angrily.

I smiled. I'd rather see Vix mad than see that frightened trembling creature.

'You were just under her spell,' Jonathon said.

'No! You've got it all wrong. I was doing stuff before

Rosamund.' Vix swallowed. 'I'd started before . . . When you're alone, you turn all that despising and hating on yourself. But I can't stop. When the pressure builds up inside me it's the only thing that keeps me sane. When I'm cutting with Rosamund it's different. Then it feels like we give ourselves strength to go a bit further. That we are powerful.' She winced. 'Oh my God – even talking about this stuff hurts. It makes me feel weird – exposing myself to you.'

'I'll help you, Vix,' I told her. 'I don't know what it is like to feel the way you do, but I do know about wanting to feel powerful and doing shabby things to make yourself feel better. I have snooped into other people's private business and kept secrets to myself. I am a total creep and I hate myself!'

Vix hugged me. 'You are not a creep. You are the talented one. We've both been mean to each other but from now on I'm going to look out for you. Now are you going to eat that bacon or what?'

Ava

BIG DAY TODAY.

The café had been completely transformed for the private view. All the tables had been pushed back so that you could see each of the installations. In the far corner, Tasha was still dabbing at the wall with a paintbrush. In another corner, a tall thin man with incredibly arty glasses was peering at my work. The smell of paint mingled with the sweet smell of cakes.

I looked round at my artwork. The doll installations were all neatly labelled. It was really happening – my artwork was going on display. It was like I was standing naked in the middle of a room full of strangers. Tasha looked up and grinned at me. 'Not bad, eh?'

My tongue, like the rest of me, was paralysed by fear so I just nodded and then looked over at the man.

Tasha stood up and slid her arm into mine as she whispered, 'That's Crispin Cookham from *Visage* magazine. He's arrived early because he's heard that this is something special. A good review from him and you've made it.'

'I don't think I'm ready for all this.' I felt faint.

Tasha pulled up a chair from one the tables. 'Sit down and let me get you a coffee.' She filled a small espresso cup and set it down.

'Are you trying to finish me off?' I asked. The smell of the strong coffee was like a punch to my fizzing stomach.

Tasha shrieked, as she looked at my clothes. 'You've made up the summer dress pattern!'

'I just finished last night. There're probably a few pins still in it.'

'It looks great.' Tasha looked down at her paint-splattered dungarees. 'I'm going to wear my black sequinned vamp dress.'

'People are going to ask me questions about where my ideas came from. Ask questions about Nan. The spotlight will be on my family. I really don't think I can do it.'

'You don't have to say anything. You can let the art speak for itself.' She waved an arm around the room. 'That's what art does. It takes a personal memory and it shapes it into something else. Something that's more bearable.'

Crispin came over. 'Are you Ava Broadhurst-Conti?' He dry kissed me three times on the cheeks. 'I love your work. The concept of the cabinets/shoeboxes linked with the exquisitely dressed miniatures is amazing. Do you have anyone representing you? Has one of the big galleries snapped you up?'

My mother's voice cut in. 'I don't think we are at the snapping up stage just yet. My daughter is still at school. If you don't mind we'll catch you later.'

Dad was standing behind her carrying a box of Champagne.

'Probably best if we talked later. There's still a lot of setting up to do,' he finished.

'Of course. I quite understand.' Crispin's voice was still polite but there was a put-out sort of expression on his face. He obviously wasn't used to being fobbed off.

Just before he turned away I caught his arm. '*Wuthering Heights* – what does that story mean to you, Crispin?'

He looked surprised for a second and then he smiled. 'Classic love story. Cathy and Heathcliff and the Yorkshire moors.'

'Good answer,' I said, smiling to myself. The matter was decided. I wasn't going to tell him anything about myself and I certainly wasn't going to let him represent me. He had failed my integrity test big time. *Wuthering Heights* was all about revenge not romance.

Dad gave me a big hug. 'The place is looking amazing.'

'We've invited around a hundred people to come along over the course of the evening,' Tasha said as she took a bottle of Champagne from the box.

Mum's face looked concerned. 'I didn't realise there'd be so many people. Victoria is in the car. She wanted to come along but she mustn't stay too long and she mustn't get overtired.' Mum spun round on her heels and left the room.

Vix

My room was not so bad
For an institution
For the first three days
I stayed in my room
Slept a lot
Skimmed the surface of
Therapist's questions
Listened to music
It filled my head
Numbed my thoughts
Didn't want to read a book
Let alone take a look at the
Dark parts
Of my heart
Thought about my life
Wished I could
Be chat show noble
And 'cured'
In next to no time
But the desire lingers

And twice
I have sabotaged my body's attempts to heal itself
Decided to go to the TV room
As I am hunkering down
In institution fake
Comfy chair
I notice that you are there
We scream and hug
'What are you doing here?'
'I was here first,'
Rosamund snaps back
'This is my third visit.'
Looking into her eyes
I know I am lost
That together
We will find a way back
To our cold, cruel
Lovers

Ava

Someone dropped a glass and the smashing sound echoed around the almost empty room.

I looked round and spotted Vix in the doorway. The noise had startled her and her eyes were hurt. She was a lot thinner now and her eyes burned brightly. Tasha came over with the leopard-print dustpan and brush and scooped it up. Vix smiled at me. She was being treated at the Abbey. She mostly stayed there, but sometimes, like today, she was allowed out. When she was better she was going to go to a local college to resit her exams.

Tasha prodded me in the ribs. 'Time for your speech, kiddo.'

'I . . . I'm not sure.'

But she was already banging a teaspoon against a glass and shouting, 'Attention.'

Vix gave me an encouraging nod so I cleared my throat and stood.

'First of all, I wanted to say how much I admire my sister Victoria, and that I hope in the coming year we can become better friends. Over this last year I've learned a lot.

'When you decide to start hating someone it is like taking a slow-acting poison. It builds up gradually in your system until it affects the way that you look at the whole world. Once the poison has taken hold, it makes you do things that you'd never usually dream of. The worst thing that can happen is that the person you decide to loathe is yourself.

'But as Eleanor Roosevelt said, no one can make you feel inferior without your consent. I'm not totally sure what she meant, but for me it means living up to the standards that I have set for myself in my heart. To try to be a creative and caring person and know that I will not always get it right.

'Most of all I wanted to do something to make Nan proud of me and to celebrate her life. These miniatures are a tribute to her. She taught me how important it is to hold on to the best bits of ourselves and let the worst memories go unnourished and neglected rather than denied or given too much power to control us.'

Vix

'Why doesn't she stop?'
I watched the hard-faced woman
Lick her salt-coated lips
And continue stuffing
Burger and chips
Guzzling cola
Feeding her hips
I wanted to look away
But I watched her
As in my mind
With growing irritation
I put her through
Liposuction
Detox diet
And colonic irrigation
Then the question
Turned in my head
And pointed itself at me
Why don't you stop?
And a part of me

Felt able to reply
I'll stop now.
In the way an insect
Landing on a petal
Takes what it can
When it can
Knows that it cannot be anything else
Lives for a day
And settles
For that

Ava

Sometimes I feel like there is a soundtrack accompanying my life. It is a pounding rhythm, high pitched and frantic. It follows me around everywhere I go, affecting every place and every person I come into contact with by its mood. Like a Wi-Fi of the soul. Everything is in tune.

I was just adding the gold icing balls to the Versace cake when he came into the café. I didn't pay him much attention. It was Tasha's turn to serve and I wasn't expecting him for another hour.

I stepped 'over to the other side', as we call the customers' side of the café, and sat down at the table.

The old man's hands were clenching and unclenching.

'She had a dress just like that.' He smiled at me.

Nan was right. He had a sparkle that shone from him.

I smiled back at him. 'I made it from one of her patterns, Victor.'

My grandfather.

Vix

For me
There is no ending
No perfect cure
Once you have crossed a line
You can't
Erase the crossing marks on your body
They fade first
But the memory of the pain relief
Of cutting pure
Takes longer
But I can change
The voice inside me
Grows stronger
Feels able to
Stand up to Rosamund's
Pressure
To cut together
At least
I can stop that
There are times when

I can go up to the line
But I stop myself
And trigger
Warning lights
Instead
So that I
Erect clear signposts in front of
That desire to cut
Signs that say
Go for a run
Make a peanut butter sandwich
Phone a friend
Text an enemy
Pluck eyebrows
Draw fake tattoos
Salute the sun
Drink moonshine
Have a gap year
Shed a tear
Have a laugh
Whisper a prayer
But most of all
The best thing
Of all is
Talk to Ava

Ava

When does your life make complete sense? I don't think it ever does. Sometimes you can piece together a series of experiences that you have gone through and they make a rough whole, like a patched up glass bowl. The pieces hold together with whatever glue is to hand – integrity, fear and lies.

I am not afraid. There are things that I've done that I'd rather forget but, if I did, then where would I be? I'd be damaged and doomed to repeat my mistakes for ever.

This year has really changed me. I've begun to see things through Vix's eyes.

It might not work out with Victor, but at least we have made contact and I can begin to understand that African part of my family and, if I'm lucky, I'll get the chance to trace its influences on me.

I'm no hero. I haven't told Mum about Victor yet. It's our secret. Mine and Vix's. But I haven't cracked up and I'm feeling less cut off.

It's going to be interesting seeing how it all works out.

And there is that small matter of meeting Dad's long

lost love – Katy/Sister Catherine. I'm not totally reformed as there is still the letter to be delivered. A misdirected letter that is burning a hole in my sewing basket. That is another story.

If you have been affected by any of the issues raised in this book, you can find further information and advice through the following organisations:

www.selfharm.org.uk

Childline
(a free helpline for children and young people)
0800 1111 (UK)
1800 666 666 (EIRE)
www.childline.org.uk

Also available by Lynda Waterhouse

Soul Love

Living with the past can be difficult,
even at fifteen . . .

Jenna doesn't want to betray her friends
and won't reveal the truth behind her exclusion
from school. So she is sent away to live with
her aunt in a sleepy countryside village.

It's here that she meets Gabriel, who seems
so genuine and different from other people she
knows. But she is wary of him at first – lately
boys have been nothing but trouble for Jenna,
and Gabe can be moody and withdrawn.

Despite her caution, Jenna can't help falling
in love with Gabriel, and the longer she spends
with him, the more deeply in love she falls. Could
he be her soul mate? He seems to be the only
one who understands Jenna and doesn't leap to
conclusions. But then she discovers that Gabriel
is living with a deep secret of his own . . .

Also available by Lynda Waterhouse

fall out

As I walked along, I felt a chill in the air.
It was September and the weather was turning
from last-minute summer into cool autumn.
Time to nag Mum for a new winter coat.
I walked slowly along the path that ran by the
side of the flats. Several flats were lit up, but
Lotte's was dark and empty. It was different
last time I was there, in July . . .

Stella and Lotte were best friends forever . . .
until one summer something happened that
changed everything.

Now Stella can't bear the sight of Lotte, and
yet she misses her. But once you've fallen out
with your best friend, things can never be
the same again, can they?